DEATH OF
AN ANCIENT KING

LAURENT GAUDÉ

DEATH OF
AN ANCIENT KING

Translated by Adriana Hunter

FOURTH ESTATE • *London & New York*

First published in Great Britain in 2004 by
Fourth Estate
A Division of HarperCollins *Publishers*
77–85 Fulham Palace Road
London W6 8JB
www.4thestate.com

First published in French as *La mort du roi Tsongor* by Actes Sud, 2002

1 3 5 7 9 10 8 6 4 2

A catalogue record for this book is available from the British Library

ISBN 0-00-717029-7

Typeset in Galliard by Palimpsest Book Production Limited,
Polmont, Stirlingshire

Printed in Great Britain by Clays Ltd, St Ives plc

For Yannis Kokkos
and Anne Blancard

DEATH OF
AN ANCIENT KING

Chapter I

THE GREAT
SLEEPLESS NIGHT
OF KING TSONGOR

Usually, Katabolonga was first to rise in the palace. He would walk the empty corridors while the night still weighed heavily on the hills outside. Not a single sound accompanied his steady progress. He met no one as he made his way from his bed chamber to the hall of the golden footstool. His shadow suggested some ethereal being as it slid fluidly along the walls. He acquitted himself of his duties, in silence, before the break of day.

But on that morning he was not alone. On that morning there was a feverish agitation along the corridors. Dozens and dozens of labourers and porters shuttled carefully back and forth, whispering so as not to wake anyone. It was as if a great ship were being unloaded of its cargo of contraband in the secrecy of the night. Everyone went about their business in silence. There had been no night at the palace of Massaba. The work had never ceased.

Over a number of weeks Massaba had become the anxious core of a hive of activity. King Tsongor was to marry his daughter to the Prince of the Lands of Salt. Large caravans arrived from the furthest lands, bearing spices, cattle and cloth. Architects had been called in hastily to enlarge the great square which lay before the palace gates. Every fountain had been decorated. Traders filed past, bringing countless offerings of flowers. The life of Massaba beat to a rhythm it had never known. As the days passed, its population had grown. There were now tens of thousands of tents sketching vast suburbs of multicoloured fabric, where the voices of children playing in the sand mingled with the lowing of the cattle. Nomads had come from far afield to be present on this day. They came from every direction. They came to see Massaba. They came to be a part of the wedding, the wedding of Samilia, daughter of King Tsongor.

For weeks, every inhabitant of Massaba and every last nomadic shepherd had come to the great square with an offering for the bride. There was a huge accumulation of flowers, amulets, bags of grain and jars of wine. There was a mountain of fabrics and sacred statues. Each of them wanted to give King Tsongor's daughter a token of his admiration and a sign of his blessing.

* * *

Now, on that night, the palace servants had been charged with removing all these offerings from the square. There was to be nothing left. The aged king of Massaba wanted the esplanade to be adorned with resplendent decorations and the whole expanse to be strewn with rose petals; his guard of honour was to be waiting there in ceremonial dress. Prince Kouame was to send his ambassadors to set his gifts at the king's feet. It would be the beginning of the nuptial ceremony, the day of gifts. Everything had to be ready.

All through the night the palace servants had gone from the mountain of presents on the square to the various halls in the palace. They carried the hundreds of sacks, and the countless flowers and pieces of jewellery. Taking great care not to make any noise, they laid out the amulets, the statues and the tapestry-work as harmoniously as possible in the different apartments within the palace. The great square was to be empty, and the palace itself was to be enriched by these signs of a people's affections. Princess Samilia was to wake in a palace of a thousand colours and perfumes. This was what the long succession of porters was working silently to achieve. They were to finish before the princess and her entourage awoke. Time was running short. For they had seen, and some had recognized, Katabolonga. They knew that if Katabolonga was up then the sun would soon rise and, with it, King Tsongor. As Katabolonga made his progress along the corridors of the palace and drew closer to the hall of the golden footstool, the agitation became more intense and the servants became busier.

Katabolonga himself felt no anxiety. He walked slowly, as he always did, to a calm rhythm all his own. He knew that he had time. The sun would not rise straight away. He knew – as he had known every day for many years – that he would be ready, sitting at the head of the king's bed when the latter opened his eyes. He simply thought that this was the first time, and it would certainly be the last, that he had come across so many people during his nocturnal walk, and that the sound of his footsteps had been accompanied by so much murmuring.

But when Katabolonga stepped into the hall of the golden footstool he froze. The very air whispered to him, something he could not understand. Even as he opened the door he sensed, just for a moment, that everything would come to an end. He collected himself. He crossed the hall to pick up the footstool, but he had barely touched the relic before he was forced to set it down again. The trembling in his arm told him, once more, that everything would come to an end. This time he listened to the feeling rising up within him. He listened and was gripped by anguish. He listened. And he knew that today everything would, indeed, come to an end. He knew that today he would kill King Tsongor. Today would be the day he thought he would never see. He understood that this would be the last day on which the king would rise, the last on which he, Katabolonga the wild, would follow him from room to room, always in his footsteps, watching for the slightest sign of tiredness, listening to his every sigh and acquitting himself of each ceremonial duty. This was the last day he would be the bearer of the golden footstool.

He stood up, trying to quiet the anguish that had germinated within him. He picked up the footstool and strode back through the corridors of the palace, his jaw set as he contemplated the obscure conviction that today would be the day he killed his friend, King Tsongor.

WHEN TSONGOR AWOKE HE WAS immediately struck by the feeling that this day would be too short for him to achieve everything that must be done. He took a long, deep breath. He knew that this feeling of calm would not be granted to him through till evening. He greeted Katabolonga, who stood by his side, and that familiar face did him good. He greeted Katabolonga, but the latter, instead of returning the greeting and handing him his royal necklace as he did every morning, whispered quietly:

'Tsongor, I must speak to you.'

'I am listening,' replied the king.

'It is to be today, my friend,' said Katabolonga.

There was something strange about the bearer's voice, but Tsongor took no notice of it. He simply said: 'I know.' And the day began.

In truth Tsongor had not understood what Katabolonga meant. Or rather he had thought that his bearer was reminding him of what he already knew, of the thing that had occupied his thoughts every minute of his life for several months, of the fact that his daughter was to be married and that the ceremonies were to begin today. He had answered mechanically, without thinking. If he had paid any attention to his aged servant's expression he would have seen in it a profound sadness, as if his face were sighing, and this might have led him to understand that Katabolonga was not talking of the wedding, but of something else entirely. Of that age-old story that had bound the two men together for so long.

It began when King Tsongor was a young man. He had just left his father's kingdom, never to return. Leaving the aged king to perish on his weary throne, Tsongor had left. He knew that his father did not want to bequeath anything to him, and he refused to suffer this humiliation. He had left, spitting in the face of this aged man who was determined to concede nothing. He had decided that he would ask for nothing. That he would not beg. He had decided to build an empire more vast than the one he was being denied. His hands quivered with life. His legs burned with the need to move. He longed to travel through new lands. To bear arms. To undertake conquests beyond the bounds of the known world. He was full of hunger. And even at night he spoke the names of the countries he dreamed of subjugating. He wanted his face to be the face of conquest. He raised his army while his father's body was still warm in its tomb, and he left for the south, intending never to retrace his steps but to survey the world until there was no breath left in him, until he saw his ancestors' banner flying everywhere he went.

King Tsongor's campaigns lasted twenty years. Twenty years of encampment. Of combat, and advances. Twenty years in which he only slept on makeshift beds. Twenty years of consulting maps and elaborating strategies. Of succeeding in his aims. He was invincible. With every new victory he rallied the enemy to his ranks, offering them the same privileges as his own soldiers. And so it was that, despite the losses, despite the mutilated bodies and the famines, his army kept on growing. King Tsongor grew old on horseback, with his sword in his hand. He took a wife on horseback, during one of his campaigns, and the birth of each of his children was hailed by the vast throng of his men still sweating from the ardours of the battlefield. Twenty long years of struggle and expansion, until the day that he came to the land of the Men who Crawl. It was the last unexplored land of the continent, the outermost limit of the world. After that there was nothing but the ocean and darkness. The Men who Crawl were a savage race who lived scattered about the land in tiny mud huts. They had no leader and no army. Just a succession of villages. Each man lived in his own village with his wives, perfectly ignorant of the world around him. They were tall, thin men, some little more than walking skeletons. They were called the Men who Crawl because, despite their great height, their huts reached no higher than a horse's wither. No one knew why they did not build homes in keeping with their height. A lifetime spent in these tiny huts gave them all a hunched posture, a race of giants who never stood upright. A race of tall, thin men who walked along dusty paths at night, bent over as if bearing the weight of the sky on their backs. In one-to-one combat they made the most terrifying of adversaries. They were quick and quite without mercy. They unfurled themselves to their full height and threw themselves at their opponents like famished leopards. Even unarmed they were formidable. It was impossible to take them prisoner because, so long as there was a spark of strength left in them, they would hurl themselves at the first man they saw and try to throw him to the ground. It was not unusual to see Men who Crawl in chains throwing themselves at their jailers and killing them with their teeth. They bit. They scratched. They bellowed and danced on the bodies of their adversaries until they were reduced to a seething mass of flesh. They were formidable, but they offered only paltry resistance to King Tsongor. They never managed to organize themselves. They never succeeded in forming a solid front to oppose his advances. The king worked his way across the lands of the Men who Crawl without flinching once. He burned the villages one by one. He reduced everything to ashes, and soon the country was nothing but a dry, empty land in which the cries of the Men who Crawl could be heard at night, bellowing their pain and cursing the heavens for the fate that had befallen them.

Katabolonga was one of their number. One of the last, probably, still alive when the king was concluding his conquests. His hut, like so many others, had been razed to the ground. His wives were raped and killed. He had lost everything. But, for some reason that no one ever explained, he did not react as his brothers had. Unlike them, he did not launch himself at the first soldier he saw and try to tear his nose off with his teeth, to bathe his hands in the blood of vengeance. No. He waited. A long time. He waited until the whole country was subjugated. Until King Tsongor set up his last camp in this great vanquished land. Only then did he come out of the woods in which he had been hiding.

It was a magnificent day, bathed in calm light. Not one soldier still fought. Not one battle raged. Not one hut was left standing. The whole army was resting in this vast encampment, celebrating its victory. Some were cleaning their weapons, while others soothed their tired feet. They talked and bartered a few trophies.

Katabolonga arrived at the camp gates. Naked. Unarmed. Head held high, without trembling. To the soldiers who barred his way and asked him what he wanted, he replied that he had come to see the king. And there was such authority in his voice, such calm, that he was taken straight to Tsongor. He walked through the whole camp. It took him several hours because the army had been swelled by all the peoples who had been assimilated and united in this enterprise of blood and conquest. He walked under the sun, his head upright. And there was something so strange about seeing one of the Men who Crawl walking in this way, calm, determined, aloof, there was something so beautiful about this long walk, that the soldiers formed a procession. They wanted to hear what the savage would say. They wanted to see what would happen. King Tsongor saw a cloud of dust in the distance, and he could make out a tall figure, head and shoulders above the crowd of curious and slightly amused soldiers. He stopped eating and stood up. And when the savage was before him, he studied him at length, in silence.

'Who are you?' he asked of this man who could, at any moment, have thrown himself at him and torn him apart with his teeth.

'My name is Katabolonga.' There was a vast silence in the army that pressed in around the king's tent. The men were amazed at the beauty of the savage's voice, at the fluidity with which the words had flowed from his mouth. He was naked. Dishevelled. His eyes reddened by the sun. Next to him, King Tsongor looked like a sickly child.

'What do you want of me?' asked the sovereign.

Katabolonga did not reply, as if he had not heard the question. For an age, an eternity, the two men stood eyeing each other in silence. Then the savage spoke.

'I am Katabolonga and I shall not answer your questions. I speak when I wish to. I have come to see you and to say to you, before all your men gathered here, what has to be said. You razed my home to the ground. You killed my wives. You trampled my land beneath your horses' feet. Your men breathed my air and turned my kind into poor fleeing creatures, who must squabble with monkeys for their food. You came from afar, to burn what was mine. I am Katabolonga and no man shall burn what is mine without losing his life. I stand here before you, here, amidst your men, and yet I say this to you: I am Katabolonga and I shall kill you. Because, by my trampled hut, and by my murdered wives, and by my burned lands, your death belongs to me.'

There was not a sound in the entire encampment.

Not one weapon clinked restlessly, not one soldier whispered so much as a word. Each of them was waiting to see what the king would decide. Each of them was ready, on a simple nod of the sovereign's head, to throw himself on the savage and kill him. But Tsongor did not move. Everything was flooding back through his mind. Twenty years of accumulated self-loathing. Twenty years of wars and massacres haunting him. He looked at the man who stood before him. Attentively, respectfully. Almost tenderly.

'I am King Tsongor,' he said. 'My lands have no limits. Compared to my kingdom, my father's kingdom was a grain of sand. I am King Tsongor and I have grown old on horseback, under arms. For twenty years I have been fighting. Twenty years of subjugating peoples who did not even know my name. I have travelled the entire world and have made it my playground. You are the last enemy in the last land. I could kill you and put your head on a spear so that everyone may know that, from now on, it is I who reign over the entire continent. But that is not what I shall do. The time for battles is over. I no longer wish to be a king of blood. Now I must reign over this kingdom I have built. And I shall start with you, Katabolonga. You are the last enemy in the last land, and I ask you to agree to stay by my side from now on. I am King Tsongor and I offer you the position of bearer of my golden footstool, wherever I go.'

This time a vast murmuring rose up in the ranks of the army. The king's words were repeated to those who had not heard them. As they struggled to understand their meaning, the savage spoke again.

'I am Katabolonga and I will not go back on what I have said. I will not take back my words. I have spoken. I shall kill you.'

The king pursed his lips. He was not afraid of this savage, but it seemed to him that he was failing in some way. And, without knowing why, he felt it was imperative that he succeed in persuading this skeletal creature. His peace of mind depended on it.

'I do not ask you to take back what you have said,' he replied. 'Before my whole army, Katabolonga, here is the offer I make to you. My death belongs to you. I say that here. It is yours. I offer you the post of bearer of my golden footstool for the years to come. You will accompany me everywhere I go. I shall keep you by my side. You will watch over me. The day that you wish to take back what is yours, the day that you seek your revenge, I shall not fight. You will kill me, Katabolonga, when you wish to. Tomorrow. In a year. On the last day of your life, when you are old and tired. I shall not defend myself. And no one shall touch you. No one will be able to say that you are an assassin. For my death belongs to you. And you will simply have taken back what I give you today.'

The soldiers stood speechless. No one wanted to believe what had just been said. No one could believe that the most extensive of kingdoms now lay in the hands of this savage who stood naked and impassive amid a great crowd of shields and spears. Slowly, Katabolonga stepped towards the king, until he could feel his breath upon him. He towered over the king. And stood motionless.

'I accept, Tsongor. I shall serve you. With respect. I shall be your shadow. Your bearer. The guardian of your secrets. I shall be wherever you are, the most humble of men. Then I shall kill you. In memory of my country and of what you burned in me.'

From that day forward, Katabolonga became the bearer of the king's golden footstool. He followed him everywhere. Years passed. Tsongor abandoned his life of war. He built cities and raised children. Commissioned the construction of canals and oversaw his lands. His kingdom prospered. More years passed. He gradually hunched over and his hair turned white. He reigned over a vast kingdom which he travelled tirelessly, watching over his peoples. Always with Katabolonga by his side. Katabolonga, who walked behind him like the shadow of his remorse, the hunched memory of those years of war. By his presence, Katabolonga constantly reminded the king of his crimes and the grief they caused. And so it was that Tsongor could never forget what he had done during those twenty years of his youth. The war was always there, in that tall, thin man walking beside him. Not uttering a word. The man who might slit his throat at any moment.

The two men aged together. As the years passed, they became like brothers to each other. The pact of old seemed forgotten. They were united, by a friendship that ran deep. In perfect silence.

'I KNOW,' KING TSONGOR HAD said. He had not understood, and Katabolonga had not had the strength to speak further on the matter. Perhaps the moment had not, in fact, arrived. King Tsongor simply spoke these words to him: 'I know,' and Katabolonga lowered his eyes and slipped away quietly as he did every day, leaving this day to start. He felt sad, but he said nothing more. And the entire palace rose, following the king. Every chamber and courtyard quivered with frantic activity. There was so much to be done. So many details to be seen to. The king was giving away his daughter Samilia in marriage. This was the day of the opening ceremonies, and the women in her retinue ran from place to place, looking for the last jewels to be polished and the last fabrics to be embroidered.

The city was awaiting the arrival of the groom's ambassadors. They spoke of great columns of men and horses filing past, one after the other, to lay down mountains of gold and cloth and precious stones in the great courtyard. They spoke of fabulous objects whose purpose no one understood but which left mortals quite speechless. Samilia was beyond price. That is what Tsongor had told Kouame, the Prince of the Lands of Salt. And Kouame had decided to come and lay everything he owned at Samilia's feet. He would give everything. His kingdom. His name. He would come before her as poor as a slave. Aware that the immensity of his riches would buy nothing. Aware that he would face this woman alone and unadorned. They talked of an entire kingdom being poured onto the streets of the city, the riches of a whole people piled up in the palace courtyard, before King Tsongor's impassive eyes.

It was the day of gifts. The streets of the city had been cleaned. The length of the route that the procession would take had been strewn with roses. Sheets woven with gold had been hung from every window. Everyone was waiting for the first horseman to appear, the first in the interminable procession from the kingdom of Salt. Every pair of eyes in the city peered into the dust on the plain to the south. Each wanted to be the first to see the distant silhouette of the horsemen in that great procession.

No one noticed that men had taken up positions on the hills to the north. That men had set up camp, and were resting their mounts. No one saw that there were men there watching, motionless, as the city made its final preparations. And yet there they were, on the hills to the north. Motionless as ill-fortune.

* * *

The day drew gently to a close. The sun's rays were turning to ochre. The swallows described great arcs across the sky and dived endlessly down to the squares and fountains. Everyone was silent. The main thoroughfare waited, deserted, to be trodden by the hooves of the foreigners' horses.

It was at this hour that the city's watchmen saw the northern hills of Massaba set alight. All at once, the crests were ablaze. The inhabitants were astonished. They had noticed no commotion during the day. Not one of them had seen the log piles being built. Everyone had had their eyes on the road and, contrary to all expectations, it was the hills that were lit up by celebratory flames. King Tsongor and all of his family gathered on the terrace of the palace. They wanted to enjoy the spectacle. But nothing else happened. Nothing other than the swooping of the swallows and the ash from the hill fires hanging in the warm evening air. Nothing else until the guard dogs on the western gate could be heard barking. This meant that a stranger had come to the gate. At each of the city's gates there was a man adorned with amulets, with bells on his wrists and ankles, an ox's tail in his left hand, and in his right hand a chain holding twelve dogs. These were the Keepers of the Packs. Their job was to drive away evil spirits and bandits. The pack on the western gate was barking, and the king, the princess, the court, every single inhabitant, everyone wondered why the ambassadors were coming in by this gate when the southern gate had been prepared for them. It was foolish and embarrassing, and King Tsongor rose anxiously from his seat, annoyed, impatient. His terrace looked down over the entire city. The main thoroughfare lay at his feet. He peered along the avenue, waiting to see the procession of gifts arriving. But it was not a procession that he saw. In the middle of the avenue there was one man, approaching alone, to the steady, regular pace of a large camel resplendent in cloths of a thousand colours. The animal and its rider pitched rhythmically like a ship on the swell of the waves. They drew closer with the languid, dignified nonchalance of the great caravans of the desert. Instead of the procession it was a single man who came into the streets of Massaba. The king waited, beginning, in spite of himself, to fear something he could not identify. Things, he felt, were not happening as they should. When the man on the camel reached the doors of the palace he asked for an audience with King Tsongor. And with the king alone. This too surprised everyone, for it was customary to present the gifts before the entire city, before the bride-to-be and her family gathered together. But once again the king assented to this unexpected request. And, accompanied only by Katabolonga, he seated himself in the throne room.

The man who came before him was tall, dressed in precious fabrics but in dark colours. He wore more amulets than jewels. No rings or necklaces, but several miniature mahogany boxes containing lucky charms hung from his neck. His face was veiled but as he came into the hall he immediately put one knee to the floor with great deference and, with his head lowered as a sign of respect, he removed his veil so that his face should be hidden no longer. King Tsongor had a strange feeling when he saw the traveller's face. There was something in him that seemed familiar. The stranger looked up at King Tsongor, and smiled. The gentle smile of a friend. He stayed silent a little longer, that the king might grow accustomed to his presence, then he spoke.

'King Tsongor, may your ancestors be blessed and may your forehead know the sweet kiss of the gods. I see that you do not recognize me. This does not surprise me. Time has wrought its work on my features. It has carved lines across my cheeks. Allow me to tell you who I am and to kiss your hand. I am Sango Kerim, and time, at least, has been unable to make you forget my name.'

King Tsongor leapt to his feet. He could not believe

it. He had Sango Kerim before him. His joy rose up in his heart and washed over him. He threw himself at his guest and took him in his arms. Sango Kerim. How could he not have recognized him? He had been a child when he left, and this was a man who stood before him now. Sango Kerim, whom the king had always cherished as his fifth son. His children's playmate, raised alongside them until he was of age. It was then that Sango Kerim had asked the king to let him leave. He had wanted to travel the world, to become what he was intended to be. King Tsongor had let him do as he wished, with regret. And as the years passed, as he did not return, they had forgotten him. Sango Kerim: he was here, before him. Elegant. Proud. A true nomadic prince.

'What a joy it is for me, Sango, to see you on this day,' said King Tsongor. 'Let me look at you and hold you to me. You look strong. What joy! Do you know that Samilia is to be married tomorrow?'

'I know she is, Tsongor,' replied the nomad.

'And that is why you have returned, is it not? On this very day. To be among us.'

'It is for Samilia, yes.'

Sango Kerim spoke these words sharply. He took a step back and held himself very upright, looking King Tsongor directly in the eye. He recognized the face of this elderly man he so loved. His feelings threatened to overwhelm him, but he struggled to control himself. He had to remain firm and to say what he had come to say. King Tsongor understood that all was not well. He sensed, once again, that this day would be long, and a shiver ran through him.

'I wish, King Tsongor, that I had the time to abandon myself to the pleasures of being in your palace once more. I wish I had time to see again all the familiar faces of years gone by. The faces of those who raised me, of those I played with. Time has passed over all of us and I wish that I could rediscover each of them, one by one, with the tips of my fingers. To eat with you, as we used to. To run through the city. For it too has changed. But that is not what I came for. I am happy that you remember me, and that it is with joy that you remember me. Yes, it is for Samilia that I have returned, as it was for her that I left. I wanted to learn the whole world. To gather riches and wisdom. I wanted to be worthy of your daughter. Today I have come back because I have finished my journeyings. I have come back because she is mine.'

King Tsongor was incredulous. He almost wanted to laugh.

'But Sango . . . you do not understand . . . Samilia . . . is to be married tomorrow. You have seen the streets of the city . . . you have seen everything around you. It is the day of gifts. Tomorrow she will be the wife of

Kouame, Prince of the Lands of Salt. I am so sorry, Sango. I did not know that you . . . that you had these feelings. So . . . I . . . you know that I love you as a son, but this . . . no, truly . . .'

'I am not talking of my feelings, Tsongor. It is no longer the time to talk of feelings. I am talking of a promise. Of a word that was given.'

'What are you saying, Sango?'

'I am saying that I have known Samilia since we were both children. That we played together. That I loved her, and left for her. I have come back for her. We took an oath. An oath that binds us to each other. An oath that has burned within me during my years of journeying.'

Sango Kerim opened one of his amulets and took from it an aged piece of paper which he unfolded and handed to the king. Tsongor read it. Impassive.

'These are just the promises of children. These things, Sango, were said in another life.'

'Your daughter promised, Tsongor. And I returned in time to remind her of her oath. Would you make your daughter betray her word?'

The king rose to his feet. His anger surged within him. He resented Sango Kerim for coming before him like this. For telling him the things he was telling him. For asking what he was asking. He resented this day, which was not unfolding as it should.

'What do you want of me, Sango?' he asked sharply.

'Your daughter.'

'She is to be married tomorrow. I told you.'

'She is to be married tomorrow. But to me.'

King Tsongor remained standing. He looked at the young man.

'You came from afar, Sango Kerim,' he said, 'to bring me troubles and anger on this day of happiness. So be it. I ask you to allow me one night to think. Tomorrow, at the first light of day, I shall give you my answer. Tomorrow you shall all know to whom my daughter is to be married. And he who is not chosen will leave. He will leave, or weep in the face of my anger.'

SANGO KERIM HAD LEFT. THE fires on the northern hills burned on. It was as if they intended never to die down. They were like vast torches dancing in the soft light of late afternoon. King Tsongor looked upon them, his face inscrutable. He had at first thought that it was Kouame's ambassadors who had taken up positions on the heights before making their entrance into the city. Then, when Sango Kerim had come before him, he had thought with delight that he too was bringing flamboyant gifts for his daughter. He now knew what these torches meant. He knew that on each of those hills an army had set up camp and now awaited his reply. Those tall flames, dancing in the distance in the warm evening air, spoke to him of all the ill-fortune waiting to bear down on him and on Massaba. They spoke to him, saying: 'Look, Tsongor, see how we climb high in the sky. See how we consume the tops of the hills of your kingdom, and know that we could consume your city and your joy in the same way. Do not forget the fires in the hills. Do not forget that your kingdom can burn as readily as a simple piece of wood.'

* * *

When Samilia came before him she did not need to ask why he had called for her. She knew straight away, as she looked on his furrowed brow, that something of great import was to happen. She watched him and, seeing that he continued to gaze at the swallows in flight and the tall flames on the horizon, she spoke to him solemnly:

'I am listening, father.'

King Tsongor turned round. He looked at his daughter. Everything he had undertaken in the last few months had been done in preparation for Samilia's nuptials. This day had become his obsession as a father and as a king. He had wanted everything to be ready, the celebrations to be the most memorable the empire had ever known. He had worked only for this, to give his daughter away to a man, and for the first time to unite his kingdom with another without recourse to war or conquest. He himself had thought through each detail of the celebrations. He had stayed awake for nights on end. Today the day had come, and one unforeseeable event had made everything falter. He looked at his daughter. What he had to say he had no desire to say. What he had to ask he would have preferred not to ask. But the flames were burning and he could not escape their encroaching appetite.

'I have received Sango Kerim in the throne room,' he said.

'The women in my retinue informed me of it, father.'

Samilia watched her father. She could read in his face some torment she did not understand. Tsongor had chosen Kouame and she had accepted him. He had spoken to her kindly and with affection of the Prince of the Lands of Salt, and she had offered herself to this union with joy. She did not understand what, at this hour, could so darken her father's features. Everything was ready. All that remained was to celebrate the marriage and to enjoy the feasting.

'His coming should have filled me with joy, Samilia . . .' Tsongor went on.

The king did not finish his sentence. There followed a long silence. Once again he lost himself in contemplation of the swooping curves the swallows traced across the sky. Then, abruptly, he composed himself. His eyes fell on his daughter once more, and his voice cracked with emotion as he asked her:

'Is it true, Samilia, that in the days when you and Sango Kerim were friends you made a promise to each other?'

Samilia gave no reply. She was searching through her memories for something that might make sense of what her father was asking.

'Is it true,' Tsongor went on, 'that you gave him

your word, as he gave you his, that you would be married one day? Did you inscribe this children's oath in an amulet?'

Samilia thought for some time.

Yes, I remember, she thought. I remember Sango Kerim and our life as children. The secrets we shared, and our promises. Is it of this that he wishes to speak to me? Why does he look at me in that way? I remember. Yes. I am guilty of nothing. Why does he look at me in that way? The promises of the past are buried today. Sango Kerim himself will come and give me his blessing. I remember. I have forgotten nothing. I have nothing to be ashamed of. What does any of this have to do with the woman I am today? I give myself to Kouame. Full of memories. Yes, beautiful childhood memories. And I have nothing to be ashamed of. She thought of all this, but her reply was simple:

'Yes, father, it is true.'

She thought that he would ask her for more details. That she would be able to explain herself. But Tsongor's expression became inscrutable. He asked no more questions. At that moment a long, plaintive moaning sounded in the distance. The sound of hundreds of zehbu horns rose up from the plain. It was the vast procession of Kouame's ambassadors announcing its arrival. Two hundred and fifty horsemen clad in gold, blowing their horns that the gates of Massaba might open and let the long stream of gifts into the city.

King Tsongor said not another word. He left Samilia, ordered that the gates be opened, and hurried down to greet the ambassadors.

THE SLOW PROCESSION OF KOUAME'S horsemen began to wend through the streets of Massaba. It lasted several hours. On every square, at every crossroads, the horsemen halted and intoned a new hymn in honour of the city and its inhabitants, in honour of the bride, her father and her forefathers. King Tsongor, his four sons, Samilia, her entourage of women and the entire court waited in the great ambassadors' hall. They could see nothing, but they could hear, in the distance, the sound of the zehbu horns drawing nearer. No one moved. The king was on his throne. He looked straight ahead, motionless, like a statue. Motionless in spite of the heat and the flies circling round him. Weighed down by his thoughts. Samilia, beneath her veils, went over and over the conversation she had just had with her father, her jaw clenched tight.

The presentation of gifts began, and the ceremony lasted more than four hours. Four hours in which the ten ambassadors opened chests, laid jewels at the feet of the royal household, unfolded shimmering cloth, presented weapons, offered standards bearing the colours of the lands that were to be handed over to the bride. Four hours of gold pieces, of rare oils, of exotic animals. For King Tsongor it was torture. He wanted to ask the ambassadors to turn back. To leave the city. To take with them their chests and trunks and to wait under the ramparts until he had reached his decision. But he could do nothing. It was too late. He could but contemplate the treasures that were poured at his feet, and nod his head, without joy or surprise. All his strength was concentrated in the muscles of his face, forcing himself to smile from time to time. But he could scarcely manage even that. It seemed interminable to him. Samilia's four brothers would have liked to express their happiness and astonishment at some of the strange objects. They would have liked to step down from their seats, to touch the cloth. To play with the trained monkeys and count the pearls in the chests. To run their hands through the bags of spices. They would have liked to laugh and to embrace this treasure joyfully. But they saw their father, impassive on his throne, and they understood that it was their duty to display the same impassiveness. Perhaps, after all, these treasures were insufficient and perhaps it would be demeaning to express joy in receiving them. And still the ambassadors continued, tirelessly, presenting their gifts before the imperturbable silence of the Tsongor household.

At last, after four hours of this ceremony, the last of the chests was opened. It held a necklace of lapis lazuli, blue as the walls of Prince Kouame's palace, blue as the eyes of his whole lineage. And blue, it was said, as the blood that flowed in his veins. The ten ambassadors dropped to their knees. The eldest among them announced:

'King Tsongor, these treasures are yours. But our king, Prince Kouame, knowing that they are nothing before your daughter's beauty, also offers you his kingdom and his blood.'

And, having said this, he spilled onto the vast flag-stones of the throne room floor a little earth from Kouame's kingdom and a little of the prince's blood, which flowed smoothly from a golden phial onto the ground, with the sweet lilt of a fountain.

King Tsongor rose. He gave no reply, contrary to what custom required. He nodded respectfully to the ambassadors, invited them to stand up, and slipped out. Not another word was exchanged. King Tsongor felt stifled by his tunic of gold and silk.

AND SO BEGAN THE GREAT sleepless night of King Tsongor. He withdrew to his apartments and asked that no one should disturb him. Only Katabolonga was there, beside him. He said nothing. He sat in a corner and did not take his eyes off his master. Only Katabolonga was there, and the aged king was grateful for his presence.

'Katabolonga,' he said to his friend, 'whichever way I turn I see nothing but war. This day should have been one of shared joy. I should have suffered only the sweet bitterness of seeing my daughter leave. But this evening I can feel the violence of war breathing behind me. Yes, it is here. I can feel it bearing down on me, and I cannot find the means to drive it away. If I give my daughter to Sango Kerim, Kouame's anger will be immeasurable. And with good reason. I would have insulted him by promising him something that I then gave away to another. Who could tolerate such an offence? Coming here with all his riches, offering his blood and his lands, only for me to spit in his face. He would raise his entire kingdom against me. He would not cease until he destroyed me. If I give my daughter to Kouame and pay no heed to Sango Kerim, who knows what may happen? I know Sango Kerim. He

is king of no country. But if he has come to me, if he has
dared to claim my daughter as a man claims what is rightfully his, then he must have enough men and allies behind
him to shake the towers of Massaba to their foundations.
Whichever way I turn, Katabolonga, I see only war.
Whatever choice I make, I break an oath. Whomsoever
is offended in this way would have every right to be angry,
and this would make him a powerful and tireless enemy.

'I must ponder on this. There must surely be a solution, and I am Tsongor: I shall find it. Such sorrow . . .
I was to give away my daughter in marriage. I had only
that left to do: to entrust my daughter for life and to let
the rest of my days flow by, peacefully. I am old,
Katabolonga, as old as you are. I have survived battles,
forced marches and gruelling campaigns. I have survived
hunger and weariness. None of this brought me to my
knees. I am Tsongor, and I knew when to bury all
thoughts of war. You, Katabolonga, you remember that
day when you stood naked amid my army. You stood
there and said nothing. I could have laughed in your face
or ordered for you to be killed instantly. But I heard your
voice. I heard the vast refrain of all those who had died
whispering in my ear: "What have you achieved, Tsongor?
What have you achieved thus far?" The tens of thousands
of bodies of my brothers-in-arms, abandoned to the
vultures along the sandy roads, they asked me too: "What

have you achieved, Tsongor?" I listened to you and I could hear only that. I was ashamed. I could have knelt before you. You said nothing; you stood there, with your eyes boring into me. I heard you. By holding out my hand to you, I buried war and I bid farewell to Tsongor the warrior. With pleasure and relief. I had been waiting for you, Katabolonga. On that day I buried Tsongor and his conquests. I buried my plundered treasures and my memories of battle. The warrior king – I left him there, in that vast encampment on the edge of the world. I never turned back to him. I remained deaf to his words. I had a life to build, with you beside me, always attentive. Now I no longer have the strength for combat. I shall not exhume the warrior king of days gone by. Let him stay where I left him. And may he rot on the field of his final victories. I am not afraid, Katabolonga. Who would believe it? I could, if I wanted to, defeat Kouame and Sango Kerim together. I could, if I invested all my skill and all my will in it. I am not afraid. No. But I do not wish to.'

'I know, Tsongor.'

'What should I do, Katabolonga?'

'It is to be today, my friend.'

'Today?'

'Yes.'

'You told me so this morning.'

'I told you as soon as I sensed it.'

'This morning. Yes, I remember. I did not understand what you said. I thought you were talking of Samilia's marriage. But it was not that. No, there was a sadness in your eyes. You already knew. You knew all this, long before I did. It is to be today, you say. Yes, you are right. There is nothing else to be done. So be it. Neither war, nor the battles of years gone by. Just the vastness of this night weighing down on me, and the restless flitting of bats. Nothing more. Your hand on me, to pull the great sheet of life over me. Yes, I hear you, Katabolonga. I hear you, my friend. You are watching over me. May your lips be blessed, for they speak what shall be.'

In the middle of the night King Tsongor went out onto the terrace. Again, Katabolonga followed him, like a discreet and dangerous shadow. He looked at the sky and the seven hills of Massaba. Sango Kerim's fires were still burning in the distance. He breathed in the warm air of that summer night. He stood thus for an hour without speaking a word to his bearer. Then he asked for his youngest son, Souba, to be brought to him.

Souba was roused from his bed by Katabolonga, but he asked no questions. He found his father on the terrace. His face troubled. His features drawn. The three of them were alone in the depths of that dark Massaba night.

'Ask no questions, my son,' said old Tsongor. 'Simply listen to what I have to say, and accept what I ask of you.

There is no time for me to explain any of this. I am King Tsongor and I have on my cheeks and in the crook of my hand as many years as you have hairs on your head. Life hangs heavy on me, with all its weight. A day will soon come when my body will be too old to bear it. I shall fold beneath its weight; I shall kneel down, and lay it on the ground before me. Without bitterness, for it was rich for me. Do not speak, say nothing. I know what you are thinking. I say that this day shall come and you must listen to me. I ask but one thing of you, my son. When that day comes, your task will begin. Do not weep with the hired mourners. Take no part in the discussions which will exercise your brothers over the division of the kingdom. Listen to none of the whisperings in the palace or the wailings in Massaba. Simply remember my words, remember this night on the terrace and do what you must do. Cut your hair. Put on a long black tunic and relinquish the jewels that you wear on your arms. I ask you to leave. Leave the city and our family. I ask you to acquit yourself of your task, even if this takes twenty or thirty years of your life. Build seven tombs, all over the world, in remote places that no one can reach. Have them built by the most brilliant architects in the kingdom. Seven secret and sumptuous tombs, each one a monument to what I meant to you. Put all your strength into this, all your ingenuity. Choose well the lands in which you build them: in the middle of a desert. On the banks of a river. Underground, if you can. Do as you wish. Seven tombs for a king, more sumptuous than the palace of Massaba. Spare neither your own pain nor my treasures. By the time you have finished this work, many years will have passed. You may be more hunched over than I am as I speak to you now. Let that not stop you. Let nothing make you forget your promise to a dead father, your promise to a king who kneels before you. Listen to no one. Silence the voices of revolt within you, and finish what you have to do. When the seven tombs are built, all over my kingdom, come back to Massaba. Have my royal tomb opened and take my body with you. Your brothers will have had my body embalmed in your absence. I shall have the hollow cheeks of a mummy, grimacing in fear. I shall not have moved. I shall be waiting for you, here, in Massaba. Take me with you. Load my sarcophagus onto a beast of burden, and leave, in convoy, for the last journey of your promise. Choose one of the seven tombs, and lay my body within it. You will be the only one to know where I lie in rest. The only one. Seven tombs, and just one in which I shall reside for the eternity of my death. When you have done this, and before setting off to live the life that you are to live, lean over me and whisper these words into my dead ear: "It is I, father. It is Souba. I live. I am beside you. Rest in peace. Everything is accomplished." Then and only then can it

41

be said that Tsongor is buried. I shall have waited for you all those years to die. And only then will you be able to cast off your tunic of mourning, put back on your jewels and embrace life once more.'

It was a dark night. Neither Katabolonga nor Souba moved. The young prince was struck dumb. He looked at his father without understanding him. Unable to reply. Concentrating wholly on listening to that voice. King Tsongor continued:

'You have listened well. I can see that. You give no reply. That is good. Remember each of my words. And now, Souba, swear to me that you will do as I ask. Swear it, before Katabolonga. And may this night alone wrap up our secret. Swear it, and never speak a word of this to anyone again.'

'I swear it, father.'

'Say it once more, that sleeping Massaba may hear you. That the land of your forefathers may feel it. That the bats themselves may understand it. Swear. And do not go back on your promise.'

'I swear it. I swear it before you.'

King Tsongor made his son rise. He took him in his arms. Tears ran down his cheeks.

'Thank you, my son, and now go.'

Souba disappeared. And once again the two men were left alone, on the infinite terrace of that summer night.

'SHOULD I SUMMON SAMILIA?' asked Katabolonga.

The king thought for a time, then turned to his bearer and shook his head. He did not have the strength to speak to anyone else. The night would soon come to an end, and he wanted to keep these last moments for himself.

'To have built all this,' he whispered, 'and to have to leave it all before truly enjoying it. Shall I be able to say, at the moment that I close my eyes, shall I be able to say that I have been happy? In spite of everything that is being taken away from me? And those I leave behind, what will they think of me? Samilia may curse me tomorrow. Her long wails of rage will be heard echoing round the palace as she spits on my name, spits on what I leave her as a dowry. She will no longer have anything but a handful of soil clenched in her fists. The gifts will have gone. There will be nothing left. Her jewels, her gown, her bridal veils, she may burn all of them over my tomb. She will curse me. Yes. Unless I manage to secure what has been denied me in life. I can sense when war is drawing near. I have learned that. It is here, all around me. You can feel it too, Katabolonga, can you not?'

'Yes, Tsongor. It is here. It is waiting till morning to hurl itself down from the hills onto Massaba. It is here. There is no doubt.'

It was as if the king had not heard his friend's words, so absorbed was he in his own thoughts.

'Listen well, Katabolonga,' the king went on. 'Tomorrow I shall be dead. I know what will happen. A period of mourning will be ordered. Everything will stop. A thick veil of silence will fall over my city. The faces of those I love will change. They will gather round my tomb. My sons. My brothers-in-arms. My faithful followers. The men and women of Massaba. Crowds of mourners will throng round the palace gates. The hired mourners will scratch their own faces. I know all this. They will all be here. Kouame and Sango Kerim will come too. It cannot happen any other way. Prince Kouame will come to offer his condolences to Samilia. Above all he will come to see her face at last. And Sango Kerim will be here too, because my death will have saddened him, and because he will not wish to abandon the field to his rival. I know all this. They will be here, at my lifeless feet. Weeping. Lamenting my death, and watching each other closely. It is as if I can already feel them. I know. I do not resent them. I would probably do the same if I were them. I too would come to weep over the father in order to take the daughter. That is why I should like you to talk to them, Katabolonga. You are the only one who can.'

'What should I tell them, Tsongor?' asked the servant.

'Tell them that I am dead because I did not want to choose between them. Tell them that this marriage is cursed because it has spilled my blood, and it must be renounced. That Samilia should remain a virgin for a while longer. Then she should marry a third man, a humble man of Massaba, someone who does not stand at the head of any army. Tell them that I would have wished for it to be otherwise, but none of what we foresaw shall come to pass. Tell them well. I insult no one. It is life that toys with us in this way. We must abdicate. Let them both return whence they came and choose another life to lead.'

'I shall tell them, Tsongor,' replied Katabolonga. 'And I shall try to find the words. I shall tell them that these words come from you.'

Katabolonga fell silent. He let the silence pervade the darkness once more. He did not want to add what he had to say. But he did so in spite of everything, in a sad, hushed voice.

'I shall tell them, Tsongor,' he said again, 'but it will not be enough.'

'I know, Katabolonga,' said Tsongor, 'but you must try.' There was another long silence. Then King Tsongor spoke again.

'There is one more thing. Take this, Katabolonga.'

In the oppressive darkness of that Massaba night he handed him something very small, which the servant took carefully in the palm of his hand. It was a rusty old copper coin. Its edges were polished with wear. The inscriptions that had been struck into it were scarcely visible now.

'It is an old coin that I have kept with me all my life. The only thing I have left of my father's empire. The only thing I took with me when I raised my first army. It is this coin which will pay my passage into the hereafter, it is only right. I do not want any other. It is this coin that you will slip into my mouth and that I will hold tightly between my dead man's teeth when I go before the gods below.'

'They will let you pass with respect, Tsongor. When they see the king of the greatest empire before them with this single coin, they will understand what you were.'

'Listen well, Katabolonga,' Tsongor continued, 'listen well for I have not yet finished. It is customary to give this coin to the deceased the very moment the funeral ceremonies begin, that he may reach the hereafter as swiftly as possible. This is not my wish. Not immediately. Keep it with you. And ensure that none of my sons substitutes another coin for it. Tomorrow I shall be dead. You have the only coin which can pay my passage, and I ask you to keep it with you.'

'Why?' asked Katabolonga, who did not understand what the king wanted.

'You shall keep it until the day Souba returns. It is only when he returns to Massaba that you will be able to give my body the fare for the passage.'

'Do you know what this means, Tsongor?' asked Katabolonga.

'I know,' the king replied simply.

'You will roam for years on end, without rest,' Katabolonga went on. 'For years on end you will be condemned to torment.'

'I know,' Tsongor said again. 'Tomorrow I shall be dead. But I want to wait until Souba's return to die completely. Until then, let me be a restless shadow. I shall still hear what is being said in the land of men. I shall be a spirit without a tomb. That is as I wish it. You alone will have the coin that can bring me peace. I shall wait for as long as it takes. There must be no rest for Tsongor until everything is accomplished.'

'I shall do as you wish,' said Katabolonga.

'Swear it,' the king asked.

'I swear to you, Tsongor, by all the years that bind us together.'

An infinity passed. Neither of the two men wanted to

speak another word. The night hung over them like a cloak. Then, at last, King Tsongor spoke. Almost with regret.

'Come, Katabolonga, it is no longer the time for talking. The sun is about to rise. We must end this. Come. Come close to me. May your hand be steady. Take back what is yours.'

Katabolonga went over to old Tsongor. He was now standing up to his full height, his ageing, emaciated body like a dangerous spider. He had unsheathed a dagger, and he held it straight and firm. He came closer to King Tsongor, until he could almost touch him. Each could feel the other man's breath on his skin. King Tsongor waited. But nothing came. Katabolonga had lowered his hand. He was weeping like a child and speaking softly.

'I cannot, Tsongor. With all my strength, I cannot.'

The king looked into his friend's face. He would never have thought that this man could weep.

'Remember our oath, my friend,' old Tsongor said. 'You are merely taking back what I owe you. Remember your wife. Your brothers. The land I burned and trampled underfoot. I do not deserve your tears. Breathe on the embers of the anger you felt then. It is still there. The time has come for it to blaze within you once more. Remember what I took. What I destroyed. We are two men in the middle of a vast encampment of arrogant

warriors. I stand before you, short and ugly, like a crim-
inal. I laugh at your words. I laugh at your wounded
people and your devastated villages. You have a knife in
your hand. You are Katabolonga. No one shall laugh at
you without losing his life. Your revenge is there for the
taking. Before my whole army. Come, Katabolonga, it is
time to bring a smile to the faces of your dead, and to
cleanse yourself of the insults you suffered in the past.'

Katabolonga towered over the king from his full
height. His face was inscrutable, his jaws clenched, and
he wept.

'I no longer remember my dead, Tsongor,' he said. 'As
far back as I can cast my memory, I remember only you,
and the dozens of years I have served you. The tens of
thousands of meals I ate in your shadow. I have buried
the Katabolonga of revenge. He remained there, in that
encampment, with the warrior king you once were. In that
scorched land that has no name. They stand facing each
other, two paces apart. I am no longer that man. I look
on you. I am but your ageing bearer, the bearer of your
footstool. Nothing more. Do not ask this of me. I cannot.'

He let the dagger fall to his feet. He stood there, with
his arms down by his sides, unable to do anything. King
Tsongor would have liked to take his aged friend in his
arms, but he did not. He lowered himself quickly, took
the knife and, before Katabolonga had time to understand,

he cut his veins with two sweeping strokes. From the king's wrists there flowed a dark blood which mingled with the night. King Tsongor's voice spoke again. Calm and gentle.

'There. I am dying. You see. It will take some time. The blood will drain out of me. I shall stay here until the end. I am dying. You have done nothing. Now I shall ask you to do something for me.' As he spoke, his blood continued to spill. There was already a pool of it at his feet. 'The sun is about to rise. Look. It will not be long. The light will appear along the tops of the hills before I die. For it will take time for the blood to flow from me. People will come running. They will rush to my side. In my agony I shall hear the screams of my loved ones and the distant rumblings of the impatient armies. I do not want this. The night is drawing to an end. And I do not want to go beyond it. But blood flows slowly. You are the only one, Katabolonga, the only one who can do this. I am no longer asking you to kill me. I have done that for you. I am asking you to spare me this new day which is dawning. I do not want it. Help me.'

Katabolonga was still weeping. He did not understand. He no longer had time to think. Everything teemed within him. He felt the king's blood bathing his feet. He heard his gentle voice flowing through him. He heard a man he loved begging for his help. He carefully took the dagger from the king's hand. The moon was shining with the last of its light. With one quick thrust he drove the dagger into the old man's belly. King Tsongor gasped and slumped to the ground. Now the blood ran from his belly. He lay in a black pool spreading over the terrace. Katabolonga knelt down and put the king's head on his knees. In a last moment of lucidity, King Tsongor looked on his friend's face. But he did not have time to thank him. Death, quite suddenly, made his eyes swivel in their sockets. He froze in one final contraction of his muscles and stayed as he was, with his head thrown back, as if wanting to drink the vastness of the skies. King Tsongor was dead. Within his troubled spirit Katabolonga could hear distant voices laughing inside him. They were the vengeful voices of a life gone by. They whispered to him in his native tongue, telling him he had avenged his dead and he could be proud of this. The king's body lay on his knees, stiffened in death. Then, in the last moments of that great Massaba night, Katabolonga wailed. It was an animal sound that shook the seven hills of Massaba. His keening woke the palace and the whole city. It caused the flames to falter in Sango Kerim's fires. The night drew to a close to the horrible sound of Katabolonga's wails. And when he closed the king's eyes by passing his hand gently over them, he was closing a whole era. He was burying his own life. And, like a man buried alive, he continued to wail until the sun rose on that first day that he was to be alone. For ever alone. And filled with fear.

Chapter II

SOUBA'S SAIL

THE CLOAK OF MOURNING FELL over Massaba at once. News of King Tsongor's death spread through every street, every quarter, every suburb. It went beyond the city walls and ran up to the northern hills, where it reached Sango Kerim. It set out along the great paved road to the south and reached the front of Kouame's procession. Thus, all at once, everything ceased. The very face of the day changed. The robes and trappings of marriage disappeared and gave way to mourning tunics and the anguished grimaces that went with them.

Samilia was devastated. Her mind foundered. She did not understand. Her father was dead. The gowns, the jewels, the smiles had disappeared. Some curse was tearing her life asunder. She moaned with rage for the happiness that had been taken from her. She would have liked to curse her father for killing himself on the day of her wedding, but she had only to think of him and her legs buckled and she cried like a child, exhausted by her suffering.

King Tsongor's body was taken away by the priests. They washed and dressed it and applied an ointment to his face which gave his features the impression of a dead man's smile. Then the body was laid out on a catafalque, in the largest hall in the palace. Incense was burned. Tall wooden shutters were put across the windows that the heat might not come in, and the body might not rot, and in the shadows, feebly illuminated by a few torches, people began to weep for their king. His children sat along the length of his body, in the order of their birth. There were the two eldest brothers, the twins Sako and Danga. Sako sat in the place assigned to the heir because he had emerged first from his mother. Danga was beside him, his head lowered. Then came the third son, Liboko. He held his sister Samilia's hand. At the far end, in the youngest child's place, sat Souba, his face inscrutable. He thought again and again of the last conversation he had had with his father. He strove to understand the reasons for this death, but he could not. And he stayed there thus, his eyes unfocused, unable to understand how a day of such happiness had changed so quickly into a funeral vigil.

King Tsongor's children did not move. Before them the entire kingdom filed past, slowly, in the half light and the silence. The first to arrive were Gonomor, the highest spiritual dignitary in the kingdom, chief of the Fern Peoples, and Tramon, who commanded the king's special guard. Then came the court representative, the palace intendant. The dignitaries of Massaba. The king's former companions at arms, those who, like him, had spent twenty years of their lives on horseback. The ambassadors, the friends and a few men and women of the city who had managed to cross the barricades around the palace and wanted to see their sovereign one last time.

Katabolonga was there, sitting at the feet of the body. And no one thought to ask him anything. He had been found on the terrace with the king, with a knife bathed in blood in his hand. He had been found like an assassin, his fist still clenched around the weapon. But no one thought to trouble him. The two wounds on the king's wrists clearly declared that he had killed himself. And everyone remembered the pact that united the two men. Some visitors, after offering their condolences to the family, even went over to him and whispered a few words in his ear. Gently. Katabolonga sat at the feet of this king he had stabbed, and, through his tears, he acknowledged their compassionate words.

IT WAS AS THE LAST ambassadors were leaving the great hall that the arrival of Kouame, Prince of the Lands of Salt, was announced. He came in, escorted by his two closest companions: Barnak, chief of the Khat Grinders, and Tolorus, who commanded the prince's troops.

When Sako saw Kouame coming in, he asked that all the other visitors might leave, that the family might be alone with the prince and his escort. Kouame was a fine-looking man, with dark blue eyes, a regal bearing and a candid expression. He was tall and strong. A sense of calm and thoughtfulness emanated from him. First he went over to Tsongor's body. He stood there for a long time without uttering a word. He looked upon the body, his face filled with anguish. Then he spoke. Loudly, that everyone might hear.

'It was not in this way, King Tsongor,' he said in the darkness with one hand on the tomb, 'that I hoped to see you for the first time. I was prepared for the joy of meeting you. The joy of taking your daughter and calling your sons my brothers. I thought that it would be my fortune to discover you, over the years, as one discovers a long tale. I wanted to be there, like your sons, to watch over you in your old age. It was not in this way, King Tsongor, that we were intended to meet. And it should not have been death which invited me into this palace, but your ageing paternal hand showing me every room, every recess, introducing me one by one to those close to you. Instead of this, your dead hand lies motionless on your chest and you do not feel my tears falling for the meeting that life has refused us.'

When he had finished Kouame kissed the dead man's hand, then he came to the children and to each of them he quietly offered his condolences. Samilia waited her turn. She kept her head lowered. She told herself again and again that she must not look up, that this would not be decent. She was overcome by a strange excitement. When Kouame knelt before her, she instinctively looked up and the closeness of him startled her. He was there, before her. He was beautiful, with well-defined lips. She did not hear what he said, but she saw his eyes looking feverishly on her. And in this gaze she understood, she understood that Kouame still wanted of her. Even in mourning. She understood that he had come for this. To tell everyone that, in spite of this death, Samilia was promised to him and that he would wait as long as he had to wait to make her his. And she felt grateful to this man for it. A tiny glimpse of life was possible. This face told her so. Beyond the pain and the mourning, in spite of everything, a glimpse of life was being offered to her. All might not be lost. She could not take her eyes from this man who told her that everything did not have to finish on this day.

SAKO ROSE TO HIS FEET to see Kouame out of the great hall, and to thank him for his attendance, but the door to the hall opened suddenly and, before anyone had time to announce him, Sango Kerim came in, accompanied by Rassamilagh, a tall thin man dressed in cloth of blue and black. For a long moment the men now gathered in the hall froze, weighing each other up.

Samilia looked on the man who had just come in. She was stupefied. It was indeed him. Sango Kerim. The past in its entirety rose back to the surface. She stared at him, and for a few moments it seemed to her that they were back in the days when he lived among them, in the days when her father was still alive. This did her good. There was something in her life that was immutable, something solid that did not change. Sango Kerim would protect and support her as he had done in the past. She looked at him hungrily. There he was, before her. In her un-happiness she could still depend on this: Sango Kerim's immutable fidelity. She had not forgotten that Kouame was present, and she had a foreboding of all the violence that a confrontation between these two pretenders would unleash. Above all, within herself, she felt the agony of hesitation, but Sango Kerim's face, quite simply, did her good. It was as if a distant voice were singing to her the childhood rhymes of days gone by. To soothe her.

Each of the children had now recognized him. But no one moved. Each of them had heard news of his return the day before. Each had learned that he had seen their father and each had noticed to their surprise how little joy this meeting had brought to old Tsongor, how surely it had propelled him into profound gloom. They had not dared ask questions. And the wedding preparations, the ceremony of gifts and the general excitement had swept aside all thought of such questions. But now, at this moment, the questions presented themselves to each of them again. What was he doing here? What did he want? What had he said to their father? These were the questions that Danga and the others wished to ask, but Sango Kerim stood motionless in the great hall, his face taut. He was pale. He tried, in vain, to hide the trembling in his hands. Since the moment he had stepped into the room, he had been watching Kouame without uttering a word. Everyone waited. In silence. Eventually Sango Kerim, on whom all eyes were resting, spoke. He spoke to Kouame, who listened to him without knowing who this man was, what he was doing here and why he was speaking to him, whom he had never met.

'You came. Of course, you came immediately. You could not wait, not even for one day. No, one day would have been too long. Of course . . .'

'Who are you?' Kouame asked calmly, not understanding what was happening. But Sango Kerim did not listen. He continued.

'You came. You did not even know him, but here you are. Yes . . . I loved him as a father. I looked on him for hours on end as a child. I would sit in a corner and watch him because I wanted to learn the way he moved, the words he spoke. Like a father. Yes, I knew him. You came to take what you lusted after, from the very feet of the dead king.'

Kouame still did not understand what this man wanted but the situation was becoming uncomfortable and, with curt authority, he said to Sango Kerim:

'Be silent.'

It was as if he had slapped Sango Kerim across the face. He fell silent and became still more pale. For some time he said nothing more. He looked on the body of old Tsongor. Then his eyes fell on Kouame once again. They slid over him contemptuously. And it was to Sako that he spoke. In a cold voice.

'I have come for Samilia.'

The king's sons rose to their feet as one man. Sako was white with rage.

63

'Sango,' said the king's eldest son, 'you would do better to leave this room, for you speak as a madman, and your words grow indecent.'

'I have come for Samilia,' Sango Kerim said again.

Kouame, this time, could no longer restrain himself.

'How dare you?' he cried.

Sango Kerim looked on him calmly and replied:

'I have come for her as you have. As you have, I have come, on a day of mourning, to ask for what is rightfully mine. Yes, with the same impudence. I am Sango Kerim. I was raised here, by King Tsongor. I grew up with Sako, Danga, Liboko and Souba, and I spent days on end with Samilia. She promised me she would be mine. Hearing news of her wedding, I came here yesterday to remind Tsongor of his daughter's promise. He promised me an answer. He did not keep his word. He preferred to die. So be it. I have come today. And I tell you that I shall take Samilia back with me. That is all.'

'You are Sango Kerim and I do not know you,' Kouame replied, seething with rage. 'I know neither your mother nor your father, if indeed you have one. Neither your name nor that of your ancestors has ever reached my ears. You are nothing. I could sweep you away with the back of my hand because you are insulting us all, here, before the remains of King Tsongor.

You are defying a family's mourning. And you are insulting me.'

'I do, indeed, have only one relation,' said Sango Kerim, 'and he, at least, is known to you. It is the man who lies there. He alone raised me.'

'He is your only relation, you say, and he is the man you came to kill yesterday,' said Kouame.

Sango Kerim would have thrown himself upon him and battered him to make him pay for what he had just said, had Katabolonga, who still sat at the dead man's feet, not suddenly spoken out in his ageing, gravelly voice.

'No one but I can claim to have killed Tsongor.'

The servant had risen to his feet. Majestic. Imposing a profound silence on them all.

'I did so because he wished it so. In the same way that I stand before you now to tell you the things he wanted you to hear. Massaba is in mourning. Tsongor asks you to bury your desire for marriage along with his body. Go back whence you came. Leave Samilia to her mourning. Tsongor does not wish to insult either of you. From the depths of death, he begs you to renounce your claims. Life did not want Samilia to be married today.'

The men standing around Katabolonga looked at each other. At first they had listened with respect, but now they were governed by impatience. They were restless with rage. It was Kouame who spoke first.

'I never thought to wed Samilia today, on this day of mourning. There is no insult in waiting. I shall be patient. Let not the king be troubled in his deathly state. I shall wait months on end if need be. And when you have eventually held the obsequies, I shall seal with you the union of our two families and our two empires. Why should I renounce my claim? I ask for nothing. I do nothing but offer. My blood. My name. My kingdom.'

'You will wait,' Sango Kerim replied curtly, transfixed with anger. 'Yes, of course. And all the while you will be consolidating your positions. You will prepare yourself for war, that I might have no chance, then, of taking back what is rightfully mine. And so I say here, before you all, I shall not wait.'

Sako was ashen. He bellowed at Sango Kerim:

'You insult the memory of our father!'

'I shall not wait. No,' Sango Kerim went on, calm and aloof, 'I shall not obey Tsongor even though I loved him as a father. The dead do not give orders to the living.'

Katabolonga looked at the two rivals. He could not take his eyes off them. He tried to understand them, to measure the hatred they bore each other, but he could not.

'Tsongor killed himself by my hand,' he said, 'because

66

he could feel war looming, and he could see no other way of avoiding it. He killed himself in the belief that his dead body would at least halt your charge. But, in spite of everything, you run headlong towards each other, trampling on his words and his body.'

'Who is trampling whose honour?' Kouame asked coldly. 'I came for a marriage. Tsongor himself invited me. I crossed my empire and his to come and be here. And my host, instead of greeting me warmly, invites me to his obsequies.'

The hall was filled with a furious clamour. Everyone spoke at once. They shouted. They gesticulated. No one gave any heed to the dead man any longer. It was then that a firm voice, a voice full of authority, rang out.

'For today, at least, I still belong to my father. Leave now. And leave us to weep.'

Samilia was on her feet. Her voice had risen above the tumult. They all stood silent. Then the men did as they had been told, ashamed to have been called to order in this way. But before he had quite left the great hall, Sango Kerim turned and announced:

'Tomorrow, at dawn, I shall come to the gates of the city. If your brothers do not bring you to me, there shall be war on Massaba.'

He went out, leaving behind him the body of King Tsongor, whose dry, gnarled hand trailed on the floor.

The hall was lit by torches. Tsongor's kin were gathered around their father for the last time, in the dense perfume of incense. They wept over the old man's death. They wept over the life they had known. They wept over the battles to come.

WHEN TSONGOR'S KIN WERE ALONE again, Souba spoke and, addressing his sister and brothers, he said:

'My sister, my brothers, I have something to tell you and I shall do it here, in the presence of our father. I saw him last night. He called me to him. I cannot repeat to you what he said to me because he made me swear to say nothing of it. But I shall tell you this. I shall be leaving tomorrow. Do not bury Tsongor. Have his body embalmed. Shelter it in the bowels of the palace, that he may rest there until I return. I shall be leaving tomorrow, and I know not when I shall return. My father wished what I tell you now. I shall take nothing with me, just a mourning robe and a mount. I shall be gone a long time. Several years. A whole lifetime perhaps. Forget me. You should try neither to hold me back nor, later, to find me. What I tell you is Tsongor's wish. I want nothing for myself. Divide the kingdom between yourselves. Behave as if I were dead. For, as from tomorrow and until the day I complete the work Tsongor has assigned me, I shall leave this life.'

Samilia, Sako, Danga and Liboko listened, and each of them wanted to weep. Souba was the youngest. He had done nothing yet. His life was an untrodden path, like virgin sand. Souba was the youngest, and this was the first time they had heard him speak in this way, with assurance and authority. He was telling them that he would renounce this life. That he was to die for several years. Souba spoke, and it was as if he had aged all at once. Each of them wondered why Tsongor had chosen Souba for this task. Why him, the youngest? It was a punishment the young man did not deserve. To renounce everything, overnight, and to leave. At such a young age. With no baggage but a mourning robe.

Samilia wept. She was just two years older than her brother. They had been raised together. The ties that bound them had been woven by the wet nurse who gave them her breast. They had played the same games through the corridors of the palace. She had watched over her little brother with a child's maternal attentions. She had tidied his hair. She had held his hand when he was afraid. And today she saw him addressing them and she did not recognize his voice.

'My brothers,' she said, 'we have one last night to spend together. I can sense that tomorrow great trials will begin for us, trials which will bleed us dry and leave us forsaken. We were all raised by the same father. The blood that flows in my veins is yours. Until this day we have been Tsongor's kin, the king's children, his pride, his strength. He has died and we are no longer his children. From this day we are fatherless. You are grown men. Tomorrow each of you will choose his own path. I can sense it, and you must be able to sense it as I do: never again shall we be together as we are today. Let us not bemoan the fact. So be it. From tomorrow each of us will carve out the path of his or her life. That is good. It is as it should be. But, this last time, let us make the most of a night we can share. Let Tsongor's kin exist as a family until dawn. Let us use that time. Time for life and for sharing. Let us have food and drink brought to us. Let us have the sad songs of our country sung to us. It is in this way, in these hours spent together, that we shall bid each other farewell. I know it. Adieu to you, Souba, whom I still love as a mother loves her child. Who knows what you will find when you return among us? Adieu to you too, Sako and Danga, my twin brothers, and adieu to you, Liboko, who always gave me good counsel. Tomorrow another life begins and I do not know whether in that life you will still be my brothers. Let me take you in my arms, each of you. Forgive me if I weep. It is because I love you and because this is the last time.'

Samilia did not finish her sentence. Souba was already

holding her to him with all his strength. Tears flowed over their faces. And like a river in flood which overflows its banks and gradually gathers in neighbouring streams, so the tears fell in Tsongor's family, from Samilia to Souba, from Souba to Sako, from Sako to Liboko. They all wept, as they smiled. They looked upon each other, as if to keep the faces of those they loved fresh in their minds for ever.

Night fell. A meal was prepared. Musicians and singers were called to sing of the homeland and the pain of departure, to sing the memories of days gone by and of time which buries everything. The children of the House of Tsongor were seated next to each other. They looked at each other. Held each other. Whispered to each other a thousand little nothings about the love they bore each other. They spent that last night in this way, in the palace of Massaba, to the sound of zithers and wine filling goblets with the sweet tinkle of a sugared waterfall.

The sounds of this last shared meal carried as far as the hall where the catafalque stood. They were muffled like the soft notes of a gentle music. And old Tsongor's body was captivated by them. He heard these happy sounds from the depths of death. He sat up and asked Katabolonga, who could hear the dead speak, to take him to them.

In the deserted corridors of the mourning palace two silhouettes walked side by side, taking care not to be seen. They moved onwards towards the music, searching through the labyrinth of the palace for the room in which they had all gathered. When at last they found the room, old Tsongor huddled in a corner and watched his children, gathered together for the last time. Their arms and legs tangled together, their hair intertwined, like a litter of puppies curled up against their mother's teats. There they were, his children. Laughing. Crying. Touching each other all the time. The wine flowed. The music filled their hearts with voluptuous sorrow.

The dead king secretly watched his children. He too let himself be filled with the soft light that bathed the room, the smells and the bursts of conversation. They were all there: his children, before him, happy. And so he whispered to himself: 'It is good,' as if to thank his children for this night of sharing. And he returned to the marble chill of his catafalque.

THE NEED TO SLEEP EVENTUALLY defeated Tsongor's children. Each of them withdrew to his or her own bed chamber and, with regret, fell asleep. Only Souba did not go to bed. He wandered a little longer through the silent corridors. He wanted to bid a last farewell to the old palace. To revisit the rooms in which he had grown up. To stroke the stone of the corridors and the wood of familiar pieces of furniture. He walked like a shadow, a ghost, imbuing himself one last time with this place. Then, eventually, he descended the imposing staircase and slipped out into the stables. The warm smell of the animals and their fodder wakened him. He walked all the way up the central aisle, looking for a mount in keeping with his exile: pure-bred, swift, full of mettle, a noble creature that would bear him spiritedly from one end of the kingdom to the other. He searched, but he felt there was something in all these magnificent, well-groomed, pure-bred horses that was not in keeping with mourning. Finally, he came to the furthest part of the royal stables, where the draught horses and mules were kept. He stood still. That was what he needed: a mule. Yes, a mule, with its slow, stubborn gait. A humble mount that neither weariness nor the sun could weaken: a mule. For he wished to ride slowly, obstinately, taking with him wherever he went word of his father's death.

He left Massaba on his mule, still dazed with sleep. He left his native city and all those he loved, leaving them to the night. A new life was starting for them, a life of which he would know nothing.

After an hour's riding, when he had long since lost sight of the last of the Massaba hills, he reached the banks of a natural basin in the course of a torrenting river. He knew it well, having played there often as a child with his brothers. He dismounted, allowed the mule time to drink and ran some water over his face. It was only when he remounted the animal that he noticed a group of women a little further along on the same bank as himself. There must have been eight of them. They were watching him without a word, trying not to make any noise, huddled together. These were women of Massaba who had come here in the dead of night to wash their linen in the pool. They knew that war was not far off, and that soon they might not be able to leave the city. They knew that, if there were a siege, water would be rationed. And so they had made the most of this last night of freedom to come here, with their sheets, their carpets and their clothes, and to plunge their hands into the chill waters of the torrent. They had at first been afraid when they saw Souba. But one of their number recognized him and the whole group, as one, immediately sighed with relief. They stayed there, motionless and silent. He greeted them with a gentle nod of the head, and they responded respectfully to this greeting. Then he goaded his mount and disappeared. He thought about these women. He thought that they alone would have seen him leave. They alone would have shared with him something of this strange night. He was thinking of all this when he suddenly felt that he was being followed. He turned round. They were there, a few hundred paces behind him. They stopped when he stopped. They did not want to catch up with him. He smiled at them again and waved to them to bid them farewell. They replied by lowering their heads deferentially. He goaded his mule and set off at a gallop. But after an hour's travel he again felt their presence behind him. He turned round. The washerwomen were there. They had walked patiently, following his tracks until they caught up with him, leaving behind the city, the washing and the river. Souba did not understand. He walked towards the group and, when he was close enough for them to hear, he asked them:

'Women of Massaba, why do you follow me?'

The women lowered their heads and gave no reply. He went on:

'Fate has decreed that we should meet on this night which, for me, is the night of my exile. I am glad of it. I shall carry within me for a long time the picture of your humble smiling faces. But do not stay away any longer. The sun is about to rise. Take the road back to the city.'

It was then that the eldest of the washerwomen took a small step forward and, with her eyes still to the ground, she replied.

'Souba, we recognized you when this night set you on the same path as us. We recognized you because, for us, you are the very picture of youthful happiness. We know neither where you go nor why you leave Massaba. But we have met you and we shall escort you. You are from the city. It would not be right for you to leave alone in this way along the roads of the kingdom. Let it not be said that the women of Massaba left the child of King Tsongor alone in his sorrow. Do not be afraid, we shall ask for nothing. We shall not come close to you. We shall only follow you, that the city may always be with you.'

Souba could not speak. He looked on these women. Tears rose in his eyes but he did not want to weep. He would have liked to hold each of them to him to show his gratitude. They stood motionless once again, waiting for Souba to continue on his way that they might walk in his footsteps. He moved a little closer and said:

'Women of Massaba, I kiss your foreheads for these words that I shall never forget. But it cannot be thus. Listen to me. Tsongor, my father, entrusted me with a task before he died, a task that I must accomplish alone. I cannot have an escort and I do not wish for one. Your words are enough for me. I shall keep them with me. Go home to your lives. That is the wish of Tsongor. Retrace your steps. I ask this of you most humbly.'

The women remained silent for a long time, then the eldest spoke up once again.

'So be it, Souba. We shall not oppose your wishes, nor those of King Tsongor. We shall leave you here to your fate. But accept our offerings without protest.'

Souba acquiesced. And so, slowly, one by one, the women began to cut their hair. They cut long locks from each other until they could each fashion a long plait. Then they came over respectfully and tied to Souba's saddle the eight plaits of hair, like sacred trophies.

Then they unfolded a great black sheet and attached it to a long stick which they secured behind Souba.

'This black sail,' they said, 'will represent your mourning. Everywhere you go it will announce the suffering that has struck Massaba.'

Only then did they lower themselves to the ground, bid Souba farewell and leave.

Day was drawing near. The mist began to disperse with the arrival of first light. Souba set off again and the wind rose, filling the women's black sail behind him. And from afar it looked like a great ship travelling the roads of the kingdom. A lone rider steering to the whim of the wind, with the washerwomen's sail flapping behind him like a long train of mourning. Announcing to all King Tsongor's obsequies and the tragedy that had befallen the city.

Chapter III

WAR

AT DAWN SANGO KERIM RODE down the hillside, with no escort, and headed for Massaba. He went to the main gates, which he found closed. He saw that Samilia was not there. He saw that none of her brothers had come to greet him. He saw that the gatekeeper was armed, and that all the ramparts of the city bristled with frenetic activity. He saw that the standard of the Lands of Salt flew next to that of Massaba over the entire city. And then he noticed an old dog skulking there, outside the city wall, saddened to have been shut out of the city. He addressed the dog from his full height on horseback, saying:

'So be it. Now it is war.'

And it was war.

Within the palace Sako, as the eldest, had taken his father's place. Liboko, commander of the city's troops, took charge of liaising with Kouame's encampment. The latter had set up camp on the southernmost hill with his servants and his army. Emissaries came and went between Massaba and the encampment to alert the Prince of the

Lands of Salt to Sango Kerim's latest movements, and to ensure that he wanted for nothing: water, food, wine or hay for his livestock.

Samilia had moved out onto the roof terrace, the very place where her father had spent his last night. From here she could see everything: the four hills to the north occupied by Sango Kerim; the three hills to the south where her future husband, Kouame, had set up camp; the great plain of Massaba, at the foot of the fortified walls. She thought of what had happened the day before: of Sango's return; of her father's death; of the argument around the catafalque; of these two men who were to do battle for her.

I wanted nothing, she thought. I simply accepted what was offered to me. My father spoke to me of Kouame and, before even setting eyes on him, I loved him. Today my brothers are preparing for battle. No one asks anything of me. I am here. Motionless. Looking out on the hills. I am a Tsongor. The time has come for me to want. I too shall do battle. There are two of them, claiming me as if I were owed to them. I am owed to no one. The time has come for me to want. With all my strength. And may whosoever opposes my choice be my enemy. It is war. The past has come back to visit me. I gave my word to Sango Kerim. Is Samilia's word worth nothing? Sango Kerim has only this. My word.

And he held to it for all those years. He thought only of that. He alone believes in Samilia, and they treat him as an enemy. Yes, the time has come for me to want. War is upon us and it will not wait.

She was lost in her thoughts, on the roofs of the palace, when Sango Kerim's army came down from the hills and took up positions on the great plain of Massaba. Long columns of men marched in battle formation. They were countless. It was like a human flood streaming down the hillsides. When they reached the middle of the plain, they halted and arranged themselves in clans, to await the enemy.

Among their number was the army of White Shadows, commanded by Bandiagara. They were so named because, in preparation for war, each of them had his face covered with chalk. They drew arabesques on their chests, arms and backs, and looked like serpents with chalky scales.

To the left of Bandiagara were the Red Skulls led by Karavanath' the Brutal. They advanced with their scalps shaved and painted red, to show that their thoughts were filled with the blood of their enemies. They wore jewels about their necks, for days of war were, to them, days of celebration.

To the right of Bandiagara was Rassamilagh with his army, a vast, colourfully dressed crowd mounted on camels. They came from seven different regions. Each had its own particular colour, weapons and amulets. The cloth of their garments flapped in the wind. Rassamilagh had been elected as commander by the other chiefs. The army seemed to pitch and sway on these great, phlegmatic animals, an army that bared only its eyes, staring fixedly, harshly towards Massaba.

Before these three collected armies stood Sango Kerim with his personal guard, one hundred men who followed him wherever he went.

This is how Sango Kerim's army of nomads presented itself. An army made up of tribes that were not known in Massaba. An army of many different colours, come from afar, standing under the implacable sun and hurling strange curses at the city walls.

Kouame's army, in turn, took up a position under the ramparts of Massaba. Kouame had asked Sako's permission to contest the first battle alone, just himself and his men. To cleanse himself of the insult he had suffered the day before and to prove, once again, his loyalty to Massaba.

The warriors from the Lands of Salt gathered to the powerful sound of conch horns blown by the horsemen of Kouame's guard.

Behind Kouame came three chiefs. The first was old Barnak, who commanded the Khat Grinders. They all wore their hair long, tumbling in tangles over their shoulders, their faces obscured by bushy red beards. Under the effects of the khat their eyes were striated with red lines, and they constantly talked to themselves, lost in the visions created by the drug they chewed. A great hubbub arose from these filthy, dusty men. They might have been an army of vagrants struck with a fever. They were all quite wild, which made them fearsome combatants. The khat spared them any fear or pain. Even injured, even missing a limb, they had been seen to continue to fight, so surely could they no longer feel their own flesh. They all muttered to themselves like an army of priests chanting bloodthirsty prayers.

The second chief was Tolorus, who led the Surmas into battle. These men walked bare-chested, braving their fear and the blows of their enemies alike. Only their faces were wrapped in ribbons of cloth. What they all feared was not death but disfigurement in battle. An old belief in their country said that a disfigured man condemned to wander the earth and to lose all that was his, including his name.

Last of all came Arkalas, sovereign of the She-dogs of War. They were strong, sturdy men but, for combat, they dressed as women. They painted their eyes.

Applied red balm to their lips. Wore every kind of earring, bracelet and necklace. They saw this as a keener way to insult the enemy. When they killed an adversary they would whisper to him: 'Look, coward, it is a woman who kills you.' At the very walls of Massaba their nervous laughter could be heard, these transvestites bearing their two-edged swords and licking their lips in anticipation of the blood they would soon cause to flow.

The armies were in position, facing each other. All of Massaba thronged eagerly beneath the walls to count the men in each camp, to look upon the weapons and the clothes of these strange warriors come from afar. All of Massaba waited eagerly to witness the brutal impact of the mêlée. Kouame's conch horns fell silent. Everyone was ready. The wind whistled through armour and lifted wisps of colourful cloth into the air.

Then Kouame advanced onto the plain. He rode straight towards Sango Kerim. When he was ten paces from him he halted his mount and declared:

'Leave, Sango Kerim, I pity you, go back whence you came. There is still time for you to live. But if you stand your ground you shall only ever know the dust and the defeat of this plain.'

Sango Kerim sat upright on his mount and replied.

'I declare that I did not truly listen to your words, Kouame. And this is my only reply.'

And he spat on the ground.

'Your mother will weep when she hears tell of the blows I shall inflict on you,' said Kouame.

'I have no mother,' replied Sango Kerim, 'but I shall soon have a wife, whereas you, you shall have as your only companion a hyena bitch to lick your dead body.'

Kouame turned his back on Sango Kerim abruptly and said to himself: 'Die then.' He came back to the head of his troops. He was red with rage. He drew himself up to his full height on his horse and held forth before his troops. He bellowed to them that he had been insulted and that the lowly dogs facing them must die. He bellowed that it was with the blood of his enemies still warm on his chest that he wished to be married. His cries were answered by the vast clamouring of the armies of the Lands of Salt. And so he gave the signal. The two armies set in motion at the same moment and hurled themselves at each other. It was a brutal mêlée, made up of horses, bodies, axes, camels and fabrics. The whinnying of the mounts could be heard, and the laughter of Arkalas's transvestites. It was impossible to distinguish the red scalps of Rassamilagh's men from the gaping wounds of the first to die. The dust raised by the mêlée stuck to the faces of the warriors as they sweated.

Samilia was still on the roof of the palace. She looked upon the jumbled tangle of warriors in silence, her face frozen. Men were dying at her feet. She could not find it in her to understand. That Kouame and Sango Kerim should fight seemed possible to her, because they both desired her. But the others, so many others? She thought of what Katabolonga had said over Tsongor's coffin. She had recognized her father's words in the mouth of the aged servant, and she did not understand why she had said nothing. She would only have had to proclaim that she accepted her father's will and that she rejected any pretender, and everything could have ended. But she had said nothing. And there, beneath the city walls, men had begun to fall. She did not know why she had remained silent. Why too had her brothers said nothing? Had everyone wanted this war? She looked on the field of battle, terrified of what she had brought to pass. This war was at her feet and it bore her name. This brutal mêlée was like a reflection of her own face. She cursed herself quietly. She cursed herself for having done nothing to stop this.

THE STONES ALONG THE ROAD began to warm in the sun. Souba rode on, pushing ever further into the lands of the kingdom, far from the rumblings of Massaba. Far from the war that had been conceived there. He rode on without knowing where he went.

The countryside had changed imperceptibly. The hills had disappeared. A great plain of weeds and ferns extended as far as the eye could see. But the further Souba went, the more signs he saw along the roadside of man's gentle intervention. First he saw low walls, then cultivated fields, then eventually the first silhouettes in that great, limitless landscape. They were bent double, working the land, each consumed in his or her toils. Suddenly a cry rang out. The shrill cry of a woman. A peasant woman had stood up and seen the mule and its rider. She had seen the sail of mourning and begun to keen. Souba faltered. In every direction he could see the astonished faces of the peasants as they stood back up. For a few moments there was perfect silence. The only sound was the clipped impact of the mule's hooves on pebbles along the road. The men and women abandoned their tools and came towards him. They thronged along the roadway to see this rider in mourning pass by. Souba then gave the sacred hand gesture of kings. The same gesture his father had used to greet a crowd, the gesture that only members of his family had the right to make. A slow, solemn sketching of the fingers through the air. This greeting was then met by a concert of crying voices. The women began to weep, to beat their faces with open palms and to wring their hands. The men lowered their heads and recited, between their teeth, the prayer of the dead. They knew. From that one simple gesture, they knew that this messenger came from Massaba, from Tsongor's palace, and that he was announcing the death of the sovereign. Souba continued his progress. Now the peasants followed him. They gave him an escort. He did not turn back but he heard them behind him. And he smiled. Yes. In spite of the sorrow he felt, he smiled, strangely satisfied that it should be so. Satisfied to give rise to the cries of a people wherever he went. The very earth should begin to wail. No one should be left in ignorance of Tsongor's death. The whole empire should cease its activity. Yes. He wanted to fill the hearts of the men he met with sorrow, the same sorrow that gripped him. There should be no more work. There should be no more hunger or fields to plough. There should be nothing more than a sail mounted on horseback. And the need to weep. The column behind him was growing, and

Souba smiled. He held to him the pride of a man in mourning. He smiled as he rode through countless villages. The whole empire would soon be weeping. The news would now go before him. Spreading. Spiralling endlessly. And soon the vast lament of an entire continent would be heard. He smiled. The black sail flapped noisily about his ears. The weeping women sobbed. It was right that the people should weep for his father. And they did, from one end of the kingdom to the other. Let the messenger pass at his slow, steady pace, from one end of the kingdom to the other. Let him pass and let his suffering be shared.

AT MASSABA THE FIGHTING LASTED all day. Ten hours of uninterrupted strife. Ten hours of blows dealt and lives lost. Kouame and Sango Kerim each thought they would enjoy a swift victory, breaking through the front lines, putting the enemy to flight and giving chase until they surrendered. But, confronted with the strength of their adversaries, as the hours passed, they had had to settle into the battle, alternating the front lines so that the warriors could recuperate for a time, removing the wounded from the mêlée and then setting off once more with foaming mouth and muscles exhausted by the effort. And even then no victory began to emerge. The two armies continued to face each other, like two rams too tired to charge but too valiant to concede an inch of ground.

When at last the sun set and the fighting ceased, both armies were in the same place in which they had started the battle. Neither had advanced or retreated. The dead had merely piled up under the walls of Massaba. A vast field of indistinct bodies, a mingling of different-coloured cloths and broken weapons. Tolorus, Kouame's ageing companion, was dead. He had continued to charge furiously, trampling his enemy, making those who confronted him tremble with his screams, still advancing frenziedly into the forest of axes set before him by Karavanath's Red Skulls, advancing like a demon, sowing panic and fear wherever he went. Until the moment when Rassamilagh saw him and goaded his camel's flanks. The animal's charge was brutal. It trampled several bodies in its path, and when it finally reached Tolorus, Rassamilagh brought down his double-edged sword with one swift motion and decapitated him. His astonished head rolled at the feet of his men and wept, briefly, for this life that had been taken from him.

Karavanath', for his part, wanted at any cost to drive his lance into Kouame's flanks. He rode straight towards him, rousing his men to combat, talking to them of the glory they would know if they killed the Prince of the Lands of Salt. But it was not Kouame whom Karavanath' met. In his path was Arkalas, chief of the She-dogs of War. Karvanath' barely had time to identify his enemy. He scarcely heard the chinking of jewellery and the screams of jubilation closing in on him. At once he felt someone leaping onto him, knocking him over and sinking their teeth into his throat. And thus Arkalas took Karavanath's life. He cut his jugular vein, and death swooped down into his eyes. His body shuddered a few times more. And he had time to hear the man who took his life whispering: 'To be so pretty, and to kill you!'

Added to all the bodies of the brave men who had left this life was the putrid accumulation of horses' corpses and the countless dogs of war that had torn each other apart and now lay with their legs splayed in the air, stiffened in death. When the combat ceased and the two armies climbed back up into the hills, ravaged, exhausted and bathed in sweat and blood, it looked as if on that plain they had given birth to a third army. A motionless army. Lying with their faces to the ground. The army of the dead born after ten hours of bloody contractions. The army of all those who would remain for ever amid the dust of the plain, at the feet of Massaba.

SCARCELY OUT OF THE MÉLÉE and still steaming from the exertions of combat, Kouame presented himself at the palace. He wanted to speak with the sons of Tsongor, to consider a strategy to defeat Sango Kerim the following day. But in the corridors of the palace he came across Samilia, and she asked him to follow her. He thought that she meant to offer him food, a bath, a thousand considerations, that he might forget the strain of combat. He followed her. To his surprise, she led him to a small room where there was nothing. No bath. No table prepared. Nothing even in which he could wash his hands and face. Only then did Samilia turn to face him, and her expression struck fear into him. He knew now that his trials were not over.

'Kouame,' she said, 'I have something to tell you.'

He inclined his head silently.

'Do you know me, Kouame?' she asked.

He remained silent.

'Do you know me, Kouame?' she asked again.

'No,' he said.

He would have liked to add that he did not need to know her to love her. But he said nothing.

'And yet you fight for me,' she went on.

'What is your point?' asked Kouame, and Samilia sensed the irritation in his voice. She looked at him calmly.

'I shall tell you.'

Kouame now knew for certain that what he was to hear would do nothing to please him, but he could only wait and listen.

'When my father spoke to me of you for the first time, Kouame,' she said, 'I listened as a wide-eyed child, drinking in his every word. He told me who you were. Of your lineage. He enumerated the splendours attributed to your kingdom, and, I confess, I was won over immediately by the picture he painted of you. The marriage was agreed upon and I was eager to meet you. My eagerness was sincere and untempered even by the need to leave those I love. But the day before your arrival, my father announced to me that Sango Kerim had returned, and explained the reason for his return. I shall not insult you by talking to you now of the man you have fought in battle and whom you must hate with all your being. You should know, however, that what he said is true. We were raised together. I have a thousand memories of games played with him and secrets shared with him. He was here, by my side, as far back as I can remember. The day he left us he explained his reasons for leaving to me alone. He had nothing. That is why he left – to travel across the world. To win by conquest what he lacked. Glory. Land. A kingdom. Influence. And then to return to Massaba. To present himself once again to the king and to ask for his daughter as a wife. We had sworn this to each other. I see you smile, Kouame, and you are right to. This was a children's oath. Every one of us has made many of them, oaths which lend themselves to laughter because they are made to be forgotten. But such oaths, believe me, become fearsome when suddenly they rear their heads again with all the authority of the past. The oath of Sango Kerim and Samilia. I would smile on it as you have done if Sango Kerim were not here, today, at the foot of the walls of Massaba.'

Kouame wanted to speak, but Samilia raised her hand to ask him to keep silent, and she went on.

'I know what you intended to say. That when the past rears up again so brutally, claiming what is owed it, that it is a bad dream, and bad dreams can be washed away. That that is what you are striving to do with your armies – to drive Sango Kerim away so that life may start again. I know. I know. I thought this too. But listen to me now and consider this. Would I be a faithful woman if I were to be yours? Sango Kerim belongs to my life. If I stay with you, I betray my word and I betray the past. Understand this, Kouame: Sango Kerim knows who I am. He knows secrets about my brothers that even I do not know. If I come to you, Kouame, I become a stranger to my own life.'

Kouame was stupefied. He listened to this woman talking and he discovered, astonished, that he loved her voice, he loved the way she expressed herself, her savage determination. He could only whisper:

'What, then, of your faithfulness to your father's wishes?'

But even as he spoke these words he was aware of their inherent weakness.

'I have thought of this, of course. And I would have honoured his wish if he had expressed one. But he preferred to die rather than choose. He left this painful task to me. I have made my decision. I shall leave this evening. You alone know of my plan. You will say nothing. You will not try to stop me. I know this. I ask this of you. I shall go to join Sango Kerim, and all this can come to an end tomorrow. Recall your army, go home to your kingdom. No one has been insulted. Life has merely toyed with us. Nothing more. There is no battle to be fought against that.'

As Samilia spoke, she grew calmer, more gentle. But the more she spoke the more surely Kouame felt the anger rising in him. When she fell silent at last, he exploded.

'It is too late for that, Samilia. Today blood was spilled.

Today my friend Tolorus died. With my own exhausted hands I picked up his decapitated head which the horses had trampled. Today I was insulted. No, I shall not leave. No, I shall not leave you to your past. We are tied to each other, Samilia, you and I. I counter your oath from the past with the promise you made that you would marry me. We are tied and I shall leave you in peace no more.'

'I shall leave this evening,' she repeated, 'and, to you, it will be as if I have died. Be quite clear about that.'

She stepped back and made for the door. But Kouame bellowed in fury.

'You are wrong! You will be by his side from now on. So be it. There is a war to be won, then. I shall come to find you. I shall break through the front lines of that worthless dog's army. I shall decapitate his friends and drag his lifeless body behind me so that you might understand that I have won you. There is a war now. And I shall see it through to the very end.'

She turned back one last time and spoke quietly, as if she were spitting on the ground.

'If that is what you wish, then so be it.'

She disappeared, clenching her fists tightly. Never had Kouame seemed so beautiful to her. Never had she so longed to be his. She believed profoundly in what she had said to him. She had prepared her speech. She had weighed up each argument. She wanted to be faithful.

She believed in that. But as she had spoken, she had felt a feeling rising within her, a feeling she could not curb and which belied every last one of her words. Once again she saw Kouame as she had seen him for the first time, as a promise of life. She had said what she had to say through to the end, without faltering; she had held her ground. But she was no longer in any doubt. She loved him.

She disappeared, swearing to herself that she would forget him. But she already felt that the further she went from him, the more surely he would become her obsession.

IN THE THRONE ROOM A terrible argument had broken out between Sako and Danga. Since old Tsongor's death Sako had been behaving as if he were king, and this infuriated Danga. The war had further exacerbated the tension between the twins. Danga had close ties with Sango Kerim and he was incensed to see his brother siding with a stranger against their childhood friend.

He too had spent the day on the city walls, watching the mêlée. When combat ceased he burst into the throne room. His brother was there, calm, dressed in his sovereign's robes. This aggravated his anger still more.

'Sako, we can no longer support Kouame,' he said.

'What do you mean?' asked Sako although he had, in fact, understood perfectly well.

'I am saying,' Danga repeated, 'that, at your behest, we are supporting Kouame, and that it is not right. Sango Kerim is our friend. Our fidelity should go to him.'

'Sango Kerim may be your friend,' said Sako, profoundly irritated by these words, 'but he has insulted us by coming and disrupting our sister's wedding celebrations.'

'If you do not want to support Sango Kerim,' said

Danga, 'then let us leave them to settle this matter between themselves. Let them confront each other in a duel, and may the better of them win.'

'That would be dishonourable,' said Sako contemptuously. 'We owe Kouame our help and hospitality.'

'I shall not take up arms against Sango Kerim,' said Danga.

Sako remained silent. He was pale, as if suffering the most humiliating insult. He looked his brother right in the eye.

'I thank you, Danga, for your opinion,' he said haughtily. 'You may go.'

Danga was overwhelmed with rage and began bellowing.

'By what authority do you assume these regal airs and behave as king? The kingdom has yet to be divided. You take all of Massaba with you. Who has granted you that right?'

Sako, once again, took his time before replying, coolly observing his brother's taut features.

'I was born two hours before you. That is sufficient for me to be king.'

Danga exploded. He bellowed that nothing permitted Sako to grant himself power in this way. The two men threw themselves at each other. They grappled on the floor like two battling insects, intertwined. Their bearers eventually managed to separate them, and Danga, with his hair awry and his tunic torn, left the throne room wiping the blood that ran from his mouth.

He went to his apartments and gave orders that his belongings should be readied and that his personal guard should prepare for departure in complete secrecy. Then he went looking for his sister to bid her farewell. He found her just as she was leaving Kouame. Danga announced his wish to leave. Her mood was as sombre as his.

'I shall leave with you,' she said simply.

It was in the dark night of Massaba that Danga and his escort of five thousand men left the city. The guards along the fortified walls thought it was some nocturnal manoeuvre, and opened the city gates, wishing the rebels good luck. The haemorrhaging of the House of Tsongor had begun. And the aged king, in his solitary tomb, heaved a long, visceral sigh heard only by the pillars of the cellar.

ALONG THE TOP OF THE hills, in the nomad army's encampment, they watched with astonishment as Danga's troops drew near. The men on watch at first thought it was an attack. But Danga asked to see Sango Kerim and, when he had explained to him the reasons for his presence, a vast cheer of joy shook the entire camp. It was then that Samilia stepped down from her horse and walked towards Sango Kerim. He was ashen. He could not believe that she was there, before him.

'Your soul is wrong to smile, Sango Kerim,' she told him, 'for it is ill-fortune that stands before you. If you offer me the hospitality of your encampment, there will be no truce. The war will be ferocious. And Kouame, like a raging stag, will not rest until he has opened your belly and delved through your entrails. He told me as much. And he must be believed. I present myself to you and I ask for your hospitality but I shall not be your wife. Not before this war is finished. I shall be here. I shall share these moments with you. I shall watch over you, but you will not have the pleasure of me before all of this is finished. You see, Sango Kerim, it is ill-fortune which presents itself to you and asks for your hospitality. You can drive me away. There would be no shame in that. It would even be the action of a great king for it would save the lives of thousands of men.'

Sango knelt and kissed the ground that lay between him and Samilia. Then, gazing on this woman with all the accumulated desire of so many years, he said:

'This encampment is yours. You will reign over it as your father reigned over Massaba. I offer you my army. I offer you my body, and each of my thoughts. And if you go by the name of ill-fortune, then yes, I choose to take that ill-fortune in my arms in its entirety and to live by it alone.'

In the vast encampment of the nomad army the men closed in to try to catch a glimpse of the woman for whom war had been declared. Sango Kerim presented her to Rassamilagh and Bandiagara, then led her to the vast tent where Rassamilagh's Tuareg women, their faces swathed in veils, prepared a meal for her and stroked her body with their perfumed hands that she might fall into a voluptuous sleep.

The men in the encampment, gladdened by this unexpected reinforcement, began singing the distant songs of their countries. Snatches of their singing, carried on the warm night wind, reached the walls of Massaba. The guards lifted their heads and listened to this music, which they found beautiful. It was only then that the news reached the palace. Tramon, chief of the special guard, ran breathlessly into the very midst of a meeting. Sako, Liboko and Kouame, roused from their discussions, looked up as one.

'Danga has joined them,' he said in one breath, 'with five thousand men. And Samilia.'

Everyone expected Sako to bellow with rage and smash the table with his blows. But to everyone's surprise, he remained perfectly calm. He said simply:

'Now there is no doubt, we shall all die. Us. Them. There will be no one left.'

Then he called for plans of the city that he might prepare for a siege. When the map of Massaba was unfolded before him, he paused for some time. He felt that this city that his father had built, this city in which he had been born and which he loved, would soon burn. His father had conceived the design and supervised the work. He had built it and administered it. Sako was obscurely aware that it would be his task, it would be incumbent on him, to struggle vainly against its destruction.

In the hall where the catafalque stood, Tsongor's body began to stir. Katabolonga knew what this meant. The aged king was there. He wished to speak. He took the corpse's hand, leant over the body and listened to what the dead man had to say.

'Tell me, Katabolonga,' asked the dead king, 'tell me it is not so. I am in the country of no light. I stray like a frightened dog, not daring to go near the ferryman's boat for I know I have nothing to pay my passage. In the distance I can see the shore on which the shades are no longer tormented. Tell me, Katabolonga, tell me that it is not so.'

'Speak, Tsongor,' the aged servant whispered in a gentle, steady voice, 'speak and I shall answer.'

'Today a vast crowd appeared before my eyes,' the dead man continued. 'They came out of the shadows and headed slowly for the boat on the river. They were exhausted warriors. I looked at their insignia, or what was left of them. I looked at their faces. But I recognized no one. Tell me, Katabolonga, that this was an army of pillagers that the troops of Massaba intercepted somewhere in the kingdom. Or unknown warriors who

came to die beneath our city walls without our understanding why. Tell me, Katabolonga, tell me it is not so.'

'No, Tsongor,' Katabolonga replied. 'It was neither a
horde of pillagers nor a dying army come to end its days
on our lands. They were the dead from the first battle of
Massaba. You saw passing before your eyes the first men
to be flayed by Kouame and Sango Kerim, mingling
together in a sorry stream of twisted, dismembered bodies.'

'So war is upon us, and I failed to prevent anything,'
said Tsongor. 'My death was for nothing, except to shield
me from the combat. They must all think me a coward,
all my sons and the people of Massaba.'

'I spoke as you asked me to,' Katabolonga replied.
'But I could prevent nothing. It is war.'

'Yes,' said the king. 'I saw it in the eyes of those
thronging shades. I could feel it in them. In spite of their
wounds, in spite of the fact that they were dead, they
still wanted to fight each other. I saw all those shades,
marching to the same steady rhythm, still staring at each
other defiantly. They were like horses, foaming at the
mouth and able to think only of biting each other. Yes,
they carried war in them. And those I love must surely
carry it in them, too.'

'Yes, Tsongor, those you love do too.'

'I see it in the eyes of my sons, of my friends, of my
entire people. This desire to destroy.'

'Yes, Tsongor. In the eyes of every one of them. War.'

'I achieved nothing, Katabolonga. This is my punishment being meted out to me now. Every day I shall see warriors fallen on the battlefield coming towards me. I shall look on them to try and recognize them. I shall count them. That will be my punishment. They will all file past me here. And I shall wait here, horrified by these cohorts coming, day after day, to populate the land of the dead.'

'Day after day your city will empty itself. We too shall count them, the dead. Every day. To see which of our friends is missing and for whom we must weep.'

'It is war,' said Tsongor.

'Yes. War. Shining in the warriors' eyes,' replied Katabolonga.

'And I was unable to prevent anything,' added Tsongor.

'Nothing, Tsongor,' replied Katabolonga, 'despite the life you sacrificed.'

Chapter IV

THE SIEGE
OF MASSABA

ON THE MORNING OF THE second day the war continued, and with it the moans emanating from a land laid to waste. Sango Kerim's men had been ready to fight since dawn. They sensed that fate was looking favourably on them. They felt it in the wind that kissed their skin. Nothing could stop them. An army of long-haired foreigners come from the four corners of the continent to bring down the tall towers of the city.

In defence of Massaba, Sako and Liboko had joined forces with Kouame. The two armies marched side by side, the army of the Lands of Salt, with Barnak, Arkalas and Kouame, and that of Massaba. Tramon oversaw the special guard. Liboko commanded the red and white soldiers. And Gonomor headed up the Fern Peoples, a body of barely a hundred men covered from head to foot in leaves of the banana tree, wearing heavy seashells about their necks and carrying in their hands huge maces which no one other than them could lift from the ground, and which made the sound of a monstrous pestle when they came crashing down on the skull of an enemy.

* * *

The two armies stood facing each other on the plain of Massaba. Before the signal to charge was given, Bandiagara dismounted from his horse. He came from a lineage in which each man was the keeper of an evil spell. Just one, handed from father to son. He sensed that the time had come for him to call on the spirits of his ancestors and to strike the enemy army with its terrible fate. He knelt on the ground and poured onto the earth the sap of a baobab tree. He picked up the dust and rubbed it into his face, endlessly repeating the words: 'We are the sons of the baobab and nothing can taint us for we were suckled on the acid roots of our ancestors, we are the sons of the baobab and nothing can taint us . . .' Then he lay the length of his body on the ground and listened to what his ancestors had to say to him. They revealed to him the unpronounceable word he must write in the air, that his evil spell might be realized. Only then did he climb back onto his horse, and Sango Kerim gave the signal to attack.

The army of nomads descended like a carnivorous swarm on the opposing lines. Kouame's and Sako's armies waited, their feet rooted to the ground, without moving. They waited, with their shields to the fore, ready to take the cut and thrust. Seeing this block of axes and swords bearing down on them, they commended their souls to the ground. The impact was terrible. The charging horses knocked men over and broke through the shields. They were drowned under thundering hooves. The attackers continued, like a wave that no force could stop, marching on over them. Numerous were those who perished in this way, torn apart by the weight of the enemy, asphyxiated under the mêlée, crushed by chariots storming through the front lines. This vast charge struck Massaba's armies like a hammer blow straight to the head, and they retreated before the tremendous impetus of the enemy. Warriors began to kill each other in unspeakable acts of hand-to-hand combat. Kouame's and Sako's men were dying in every direction. They were afraid. The sight of this charge crushing their forces had allowed terror to blossom within them. They were less sure of themselves in combat. Their bodies hesitated. They scanned the battlefield for some form of support while, opposite them, the nomad army continued to advance, spurred on by its prodigious sense of rage. Only the Khat Grinders fought with courage, the drugs that ran through their blood having dissipated any fear. They thought of nothing other than striking blows at the enemy.

* * *

Arkalas's She-dogs of War fought furiously, but a horrible fate awaited them. Bandiagara encompassed them in one loathing stare, these thousands of men parading as women, these men who sickened him, and he drew in the air the secret word that his ancestors had entrusted to him. Their minds were suddenly veiled in confusion. They looked at each other and saw in their own brothers the enemy that must be exterminated. And so the She-dogs threw themselves at each other, convinced that they were continuing the battle, while the real enemy stood by. They provided a horrifying spectacle, an army tearing itself to pieces. Arkalas's men, dressed and preened in preparation for war, now threw themselves at each other and bit each other to death. They laughed insanely as they killed, sometimes even dancing on the body of some childhood friend. Arkalas himself, like a demented ogre, looked everywhere for his kin that he might rip them open and drink their blood. When the rest of the army realized that Arkalas's men were not only no longer fighting but, worse still, were killing each other, panic ran up and down the front line. Then every man began to run to escape death. Kouame's appalled screams could hold no one back. Each man could think only of saving his own life. The horsemen goaded the flanks of their mounts. Warriors threw their shields and weapons to the ground that they might run more swiftly. As one, they hurled themselves at the gates of Massaba to take shelter. Tramon perished, stopped in his flight by Sango Kerim, who drove his slender lance right into his back. The life slipped out of him and he slumped to the ground, with the spear standing perfectly straight from his spine.

The army was routed, driven on by the swords slashing at their heels, mowing down those who were too slow. Arkalas alone, a grotesque and pathetic combatant, still fought. He killed the last of his men with a great blow of his mace which shattered the bones in the man's neck. Only then did Bandiagara's spell dissipate and Arakalas regained his senses. At his feet he saw dozens of men he knew. He was perched on a mountain of bodies, and the blood splattered all over his face had the familiar taste of those dear to him. He would have stayed there, crushed by the terror of it, shaking his head in disbelief, his face bathed in tears, had Gonomor not taken him with him, escorted by the Fern Peoples, and led him to safety within the walls of Massaba.

When the last fleeing soldier was inside Massaba and the huge gate had been closed, a great roar of joy reverberated around the plain. Half the men of Massaba had been massacred. Within the city walls, no one spoke. The warriors caught their breath. When, at last, they could breathe again, they began to weep. Silently. Their hands, legs and heads trembled as only the bodies of the vanquished tremble.

IN THE PANIC OF THE retreat, Kouame's men had abandoned their encampment on the southern hills of Massaba, and it was with disgust that they watched from the top of the city walls as Rassamilagh's horsemen rode round the settlement and took possession of their tents, supplies and livestock. Everything was lost. There was nothing more they could do. Cheers of joy carried to them from the encampment and completed their sense of desolation. Arkalas in particular was painful to behold. He wandered aimlessly along the ramparts, muttering the names of those dear to him. He howled in pain and scratched his own skin raw, cursing the heavens. He retched and spewed over the city walls at the very thought of what he had done. He smacked his forehead against the walls, howling.

'Bandiagara, prepare to suffer. Bandiagara, you will beg to die when I hold you in my hands. May the heavens grant that from this moment I shall be the most fearsome scourge to my enemies. I shall be he who no longer fears their blows and never retreats.'

*　*　*

Massaba was crushed by a profound torpor. The weight of misfortune suffocated all thought, every mind. The men no longer wished for anything. They no longer had any strength. They would all have succumbed to the lethargy of despair had Barnak, the aged Khat Grinder, not stood up and wakened them from their torpor. He spoke of everything that remained to be done. Of the time that was so precious to them, and of the need to organize themselves for combat the following day. Then, driven on by this ageing, long-haired warrior with his rolling, drug-dazed eyes, the city of Massaba awoke and prepared for the siege. Every inhabitant participated. Long lines of men and women worked through the night. The gates were fortified, breaches in the walls were sealed, rationing was organized. Stores of food were laid out in the vast cellars of the palace: wheat, barley, jars of oil, flour. The cellars of houses were converted into water reservoirs. The whole city began to look like a fortified stronghold. The streets clattered with the clinking of weapons and the hammering of horses' hooves on the cobbles. Preparations were being made for a long siege, a siege that would carve hollows into the faces of the inhabitants and create cracks in the city walls with the hunger of it.

THAT NIGHT, AFTER RASSAMILAGH'S RAID on the southern hills, a meeting was organized in the nomad camp. The spoils of war were handed out. Then, while Sango Kerim, Danga and Bandiagara drank a sweet spirit of sand myrtles, Rassamilagh rose to his feet and announced:

'Sango Kerim, the sweet spirit you drink is the spirit of victory, and I bless this day that saw our army break through the enemy lines. The time has now come to decide what we shall do tomorrow. For my part, I shall state my opinion clearly. I have pondered this at length. Let us raise camp and leave these lands. We have got what we wanted. We have humiliated our adversary in combat. You have won the woman you came to find. We can expect nothing more from this war.'

Bandiagara leapt from his seat and replied to Rassamilagh.

'How can you say such a thing? What brand of warrior are you that you can give up the spoils when you have won the victory? Massaba is there. It is ours. The prize awaits us. For my part, I say this: I shall await the day when I am given what is owed to me, and receive it from the hand of Sango Kerim. And I shall do my utmost to ensure that that day shall be tomorrow.'

'He is right,' added Danga. 'The worst is behind us. It only remains for us to take Massaba. I shall open the gates of this city for you with my own hands.'

'I shall not fight for the spoils,' Rassamilagh went on. 'I shall fight because Sango Kerim has asked me to. He came here to find a woman who had been promised to him. That woman is now among us. I did not come here to bring down a city. From this day, another war begins. And I do not know what we can expect of it.'

'Power,' said Danga, coldly.

Rassamilagh gazed at Danga at length, without hatred, but with detachment.

'I do not know you, Danga,' he said at last. 'We are allied by the friendship we both bear Sango Kerim, but it is not for you that I fight. What is it to me whether you or your brother reigns over Massaba? Do not forget this, Danga. I do nothing for you.'

It was then that Sango Kerim spoke.

'What would it say of me, Rassamilagh, if I were to leave on this night, stealing away the woman I came for as if I were a thief? She is the daughter of King Tsongor. I do not intend to give her nomadic paths in the desert as a dowry, but her own city reconquered. She would not know how to live anywhere else. Her father would curse me between his dead man's teeth if he learned that I had made a wandering nomad of his heiress. This city is ours. There is no victory if we do not succeed in taking it.'

'I have said what I had to say and I do not regret having spoken,' replied Rassamilagh. 'None of your arguments persuades me. It is merely a taste for victory that I hear from your mouths. I recognize it. But I can see that I am alone in thinking of leaving. Fear not. I shall stay with you. Rassamilagh is not a coward. But remember this night when everything could have ended, and pray that we may never regret it nor the sweetness of the myrtles.'

SO IT WAS THAT THE war continued. The following morning the nomad army confronted the walls of Massaba once more. The men in the city massed along the ramparts. All night they had been preparing cauldrons of hot oil and murderous stones to drive back the enemy assault.

Just as Sango Kerim was about to give the signal to charge, shouts rang out from the crowd of warriors.

'The Army of Ashes, the Army of Ashes!'

Every man turned to look. A troop of men was indeed appearing along the furthest hilltop. It was Orios, with his Army of Ashes, a savage people who lived in the high mountains of Krassos. They had promised their support to Sango Kerim but had never joined him. Theirs was a fearsome army of two thousand men. Sango Kerim smiled and stood up in his stirrups to greet Orios. The horsemen of Ashes were indeed joining them, but as they drew closer, murmurings of disbelief ran through the army. This was not Orios's great army which was presented to them but a handful of men covered in dust. There were some one hundred of them. Barely that. Their faces were gaunt, their weapons blunted – a small troop of bewildered horsemen. Orios came right up to Sango Kerim and spoke to him, saying:

'Greetings, Sango Kerim. Do not look at me in that way. I know that it was not this handful of men that you were expecting. I shall tell you, if you wish it and if the gods mean me to live long enough, of the trials we have endured to reach you here. You should know only this: that it was at the head of my whole army that I left the peaks of Krassos and that all I am left with today are those you see here. But the men you see have undergone so much combat, have endured so much privation and pain to come this far that there is nothing that can now stop them. Every one of them, believe me, is worth a hundred of your men.'

'I greet you, Orios, you and each of your warriors. I shall listen hungrily to the account of your trials once we have sacked Massaba. For now, go to the encampment. Rest. Let your mounts graze. And wait for the sun to set and for us to return from combat. Then we shall drink together the wine of brothers, and I myself shall wash your feet, bruised by the territories you have crossed, that I might thank you for your loyalty.'

'I have not crossed an entire continent,' replied Orios, 'in order to sleep while you do battle. These hundred men, as I said, have become savage beasts and nothing can now weary them. Show us the city walls we are to break down, and let the hour of combat strike for us.'

Sango Kerim agreed, and had the troop of Ashes drawn up beside him. Then, armed with this new support, he launched himself across the plain, taking with him thousands of men, swallowing up the land beneath their feet.

The bulk of the troops hurried towards the central gate in the hope that it would give way. Meanwhile Danga, who knew the city better than anyone, tried to penetrate through the old doorway in the Tower. Everything seemed to be smiling on the nomad armies. While the combatants inside the city thronged along the eastern wall to try to check the wave of attackers, Danga and his personal guard had no trouble breaking down the worm-eaten door to the Tower, and fighting began in the first few streets of the city. The news reached Sako and Kouame immediately. They had only a few men to counter this attack. To withdraw troops from the walls would be to risk being overrun by the enemy. So they commanded old Barnak and his drugged warriors to stand up to Danga unaided. The Khat Grinders were joined by Arkalas who, since combat had resumed, seemed to have become a furious, maddened demon.

The battle was horrifying and lasted most of the day. Arkalas and Barnak offered tenacious resistance to Danga's feverish onslaught. The wall they formed seemed insurmountable. Danga fumed and raged. The palace was there, barely five hundred paces from him. He could see it. He had only to pass this handful of men to take the city back from his brother. But there was nothing to be done. Arkalas fought like a madman. He harried his enemies. Provoked them. Came forward and plucked them from the ranks if they hesitated before attacking. Old Barnak, intoxicated by his drug, seemed to dance among the corpses. Danga, very gradually, retreated. Then, furious not to have succeeded in penetrating Massaba, he ordered his men to send flaming arrows into the nearby houses. He set fire to whatever he could, and the fire, like gangrene, spread from roof to roof, setting loose vast billows of smoke in every direction. The terrified inhabitants ran from one place to another with paltry containers of water. Arkalas and Barnak had driven Danga back and sealed the breach, but now the city was being eaten away by fire.

It was when they had climbed back into the hills at nightfall that Sango Kerim and his men realized the city was burning. They watched the spectacle of thousands of men trying to fight flames taller than the towers of the city. The heavy layers of smoke that rose up from Massaba bore with them the sad smell of the houses swallowed up in the blaze. Night was falling and Massaba screamed like a man whose face is on fire.

When Danga finally arrived, happy, in spite of everything, to have sown such terror in the city, Samilia was waiting for him. Motionless, her eyes locked onto him. When he stepped down from his horse she slapped him, before all his men and before the army chiefs gathered there.

'Is this how you pay homage to your dead father? I spit on you for thinking such stupid thoughts.'

Sango Kerim, mortified by the spectacle of flames devouring the city of his childhood, promised Samilia that no attack would be launched so long as the inhabitants of Massaba had not overcome the fire. But a mask of pain had fallen over Samilia's face, a mask that nothing could remove.

IN THE DEATH CHAMBER IN the palace, Katabolonga had come down to be beside the king's body. He applied dampened strips of cloth to the corpse, that his skin might not blister or eventually catch fire. And, at first, King Tsongor wondered what it was that Katabolonga wanted of his old dead body.

'What use is it to you, Katabolonga, doing what you are doing?' he asked. 'Are you stroking my corpse? Are you covering me with oil? I feel nothing. And there is no need for you to take care of me in this way. Unless time has passed more quickly than I thought, and my body is beginning to decompose in spite of the balms and unguents. What is it you are doing, Katabolonga, and why do you not answer me?'

Katabolonga heard old Tsongor's voice but could not reply. His lips trembled. He kept his head lowered and continued to dampen the body. It was hot, and sweat ran down his forehead. These droplets of sweat mingled with the tears he was unable to hold back. They fell onto the aged king's body, refreshing the sovereign's remains. Tsongor was troubled once again, by this silence.

'Why do you not speak to me, Katabolonga? What is happening in Massaba?'

Katabolonga could hold his tongue no longer.

'If your skin could feel the heat and the cold, you would not need to ask, Tsongor. If you could breathe the air in this chamber, you would have nothing to learn from me.'

'I have no senses, Katabolonga. Speak. Tell me.'

'Everything is burning, Tsongor. Massaba is in flames. And the heat of the fire causes me to cough even here. That is why I am busying myself over you. You feel nothing. Your skin is burning hot, like the stone around you. Soon you would blister and burst into flames if I did not do what I must. I am covering your body with dampened cloth. I am sprinkling water over you, that you might not catch light.'

The aged king could not speak. From the depths of his darkness he closed his eyes. It seemed to him now that he could smell the fire. He let this smell pervade him completely. Yes. He was now surrounded by thick smoke, facing the tall flickering flames. And the smell of burning all around him, he could sense that too. Then he spoke again, very quietly, like a sleepwalker devastated by the dream he is having.

'Yes. I see. Everything is burning. The flames were small at first but the wind has risen and now they leap from one roof to the other, eating through the city one district at a time. My palace has fallen victim to it. The fire is licking along the walls, catching hold of the wall-hangings, sending them crumbling to the floor in a cloud of sparks. Yes, I see. From the terrace of the palace, a vast inferno is spreading at my feet. The houses collapse with a great sighing of wood. In the working men's quarters there is already almost nothing left. The fire spread there more quickly than anywhere else. The men had built very few walls of stone there, just a mass of wooden shacks, little workshops and tents. Everything has disappeared. Yes, I see the men fighting and battling against the walls of fire. Everything is burning and everything is groaning and creaking. My city. My poor city. I built it, year after year. I conceived its design myself. I supervised the work. I trod up and down its streets until I knew every corner and recess. It was the image of my own face etched in stone. If it is burning, Katabolonga, if it is burning, then my whole life is being borne away in the smoke. I wanted to build an empire that knew no limits, to build a capital that would plunge my father and his tiny kingdom into distant prehistory. If Massaba is burning, then I am reduced to his stature again. I, like him, am the tyrant of an ugly, cramped territory. If it is burning, I have given nothing to those I love.'

'You have given, Tsongor, but your gifts are being burned,' replied Katabolonga.

King Tsongor fell silent again. Katabolonga had finished his work. The dead king's body was now damp and out of danger. It was then that Katabolonga heard Tsongor speaking again. But his voice was far off. He had to lean over the dead man's face to hear what he murmured.

'Now,' said Tsongor, 'now I see them. They are coming. They are here. The first of the burned of Massaba. Women. Children. Whole families with their faces burned to ashes. These are my people. I recognize them. The fire has killed them. Their skin is ravaged, their eyes expressionless. I am king of a burned people, Katabolonga. Do you see them, as I do? You were wrong, Katabolonga. It is not on me that you should put the strips of cloth. It is not my skin that needs quenching. It is the skin of the burned, the burned of Massaba. It is them you should be stroking. Do you see them? I have nothing. And you, you poor souls, do you see? I have nothing to offer you. But I weep over you, the burned of Massaba. And I place each of my tears delicately on your tortured bodies in the hope that they might relieve your suffering.'

Tsongor's voice disappeared. Katabolonga stood up. Then he saw that the king's corpse was weeping, great tears of water to relieve the skin of the burned. Outside, the city continued to twist and gnarl in the flames.

For a week the houses burned. And for a week the war was suspended. The besieged battled, day and night, against the fire. And the nomad army watched, speechless, the spectacle of this splendour in stone being consumed by fire. On the seventh day the flames were at last brought under control. The inhabitants of Massaba all wore a black mask of smoke on their faces. Their hair singed, their skin scalded by the heat of the flames, and their clothes covered in soot, they were exhausted. Whole streets were covered in embers. Houses had collapsed. Amid the crumbling heaps of stone were the silhouettes of blackened beams. Part of the food stores had been lost. There was nothing left. Nothing but the terrifying memory of the gigantic flames which, for many days to come, would continue to dance in the minds of the exhausted inhabitants.

FAR FROM THE BLAZE IN Massaba, Souba continued on his way. He was drawing near to Saramine, the hanging city. He could already see its tall white walls. After Massaba, Saramine was the second jewel in the kingdom, an elegant city built of pale stone which took on a rosy glow in the evening light. A city built above high cliffs overlooking the sea.

Old Tsongor had loved this city. He had often stayed there, without ever giving orders for any changes to be made to it. Throughout his life he had, quite intentionally, distanced himself from the running of the citadel so that nothing in it should bear his mark. He did not wish to appropriate it for himself. The citadel of Saramine seemed beautiful to him because there was nothing of himself in it. That is why he liked to come here. He felt like a stranger here, curious about each of its buildings, admiring the architecture, the quality of the light, and that peculiar elegance which he watched over as a sovereign but which owed nothing to him. He had given this city to one of his oldest companions: Manongo. But after a few years' reign Manongo died, taken away by a fever. Custom dictated that Tsongor should name another war chief to lead it, another long-term companion, to thank him for his loyalty, and to show everyone the kind of gifts Tsongor bestowed on those who followed him. But that was not what he did. Manongo, thanks to his gentleness, had succeeded in earning the affection of the people of Saramine. He was venerated with passion. He had administered his town intelligently and with generosity. Tsongor himself came to attend Manongo's obsequies. He wept with the people of Saramine. He paced silently up and down the streets of the citadel in the heat, amid the weeping crowd. He understood how very much his old brother-in-arms was loved by this city, and decided that the power should pass to Shalamar, Manongo's widow. He knew her well. She too had been with them in all their battles, following her husband everywhere – through long campaigns, in magnificent palaces, sharing his fears through the years of war and in the prosperity of the years of power. Shalamar had never asked for anything. She was the first and only woman in the kingdom to be raised to such a rank. The people of Saramine greeted this decision with joy. Years passed and Shalamar looked after the city lovingly. Every time Tsongor came to visit, he did so with humility, thinking of himself as a guest and not as a king. He had always wanted it thus, that Saramine should grow in stature in an atmosphere of benevolent freedom.

* * *

By the time Souba entered the hanging citadel, news of his father's death had gone before him. It was as if the city were waiting for him. In the main thoroughfare, on the squares, at every little crossroads, the crowds gathered to watch Souba approaching. Every kind of activity had ceased. No one even spoke.

It was on the high terrace of the palace that Shalamar greeted her guest. The terrace looked down over the sea from a terrifying cliff where sea-birds soared. Shalamar was dressed in black. When she saw Souba she rose from her throne and knelt on the ground. The king's son was surprised by this gesture. He had learned, from his father, that Shalamar was a great queen. He saw before him a woman much aged, hunched over by the years, and this proud woman was kneeling before him. He understood that it was before the shadow of Tsongor that she prostrated herself, and he helped her, gently and attentively, to her feet, and led her back to her throne. She then offered him the condolences of her people. And, as Souba said nothing, she called for a singer who sang two funeral songs for them. On that terrace overlooking the world, with the sea beating against the rocks at the foot of the cliff, Souba let the singing and his sorrow steal over him. He wept. It was as if his father had died that day, all over again. The time that had passed since he left Massaba had appeased nothing. The pain was there. Suffocating.

It seemed to him that he would never be able to master it. Shalamar let him weep. She waited patiently. She too remembered all the moments in her life linked with Tsongor. Then, after a time, she asked him to come closer to her, took both his hands as she would have a child's, and asked him in a gentle motherly voice what she could do for him. He could ask anything of her, in the name of his father, in the name of his memory. Saramine would do everything he asked.

Souba asked that eleven days of mourning be arranged in the city. That sacrifices be made. He asked that Saramine might share in the mourning with Massaba, its sister in stone. Then he fell silent again. He expected Shalamar to give orders immediately, but she did nothing. She looked at the silhouettes of the towers and the terraces outlined against the mingled blue of the sky and the sea. Then she turned to Souba. Her face had changed. It was not that of a saddened old woman. Something harder and more aloof now emanated from her features. It was then that she began to talk in a cavernous voice which bore with it a whole lifetime of suffering and tenderness.

'Listen, Souba, listen carefully to what I have to say to you. Listen to me as a son listens to his mother. I shall do what you have asked of me in the name of Tsongor. But that is not what I was asking. You need not give orders of any kind for mourning to grip the city of Saramine. Tsongor is dead and, to me, it is as if a whole part of my life has slipped gently into the sea. We shall weep for him. And our mourning shall last more than eleven days. Leave that to us. Leave us to organize the funeral ceremonies as we see fit. You will see that the city will weep for your father as it should. Listen, Souba, listen to Shalamar. I knew your father. If he sent you out onto the roads of his kingdom it was not to make of you the messenger of his death. There is no need for your presence in order for the whole kingdom to grimace in sorrow. I knew your father. He could not have thought that it would require the vigilance of one of his sons for Saramine to weep for him. There was something else that he expected of you. Leave the mourning to us, Souba. We shall acquit ourselves of it. Leave it behind you here, in Saramine. Your father did not raise you that you might weep. It is time you rid yourself of mourning. Do not let my words anger you. I too have known the pain of loss more than once. I too have known the voluptuous vertigo it brings. You must force yourself to take off your mask of tears, and leave it at your feet. Do not succumb to the arrogance of one who has lost everything. It is his son whom Tsongor needs now, not a hired mourner, a weeping woman.'

She fell silent. Souba's head was spinning. While

Shalamar talked he had wanted to interrupt her several times. He felt insulted. But he had listened to the end, for there was an authority in her voice, a natural penetrating authority which told him she was right. He stayed before her, unable to speak. This aged woman with the lined hands, this ageing sovereign had struck him with her hoarse old voice as surely as if she had slapped him.

'You are right, Shalamar,' he replied. 'Your words cause my cheeks to burn but I know that you speak the truth. Yes, Shalamar. I leave to you the mourning and the weeping women. Make of it what you will. May Saramine do as it sees fit. As it always has. You are right. Tsongor did not send me here to weep. He asked me to build seven tombs throughout his kingdom. Seven tombs to speak of the man he was. It is here that I wish to build the first tomb, in this city that he loved. Yes, it is here that my vast building works shall begin. You are right, Shalamar. The stone is calling to me. I leave the weeping to you.'

Slowly, he folded the long black sail that the women of Massaba had given him, and he put it into the hands of the aged queen. Her face once again became that of a mother. She smiled before this young man who had had the strength to listen to her. She took the sail, then waved Souba closer still to her and, as she kissed his forehead, she whispered:

'Do not be afraid, Souba. Do what you have to do. I shall weep for you. All of Saramine will weep for you. You can go in peace. And confront the stone that calls you.'

THE SIEGE OF MASSABA CONTINUED. Every day, while Kouame and Sako's warriors strove to drive back the enemy on the ramparts, the inhabitants cleared the rubble, cleaned the streets and dug from ruins that were still warm anything spared by the flames. Great armfuls of rubble, ash and fragmented belongings were used to drive back the enemy. They were flung with full force over the assailants. Massaba spewed long streams of dust and ash from the tops of its walls.

Within the walls life was well organized. Everything was subject to the economies of war. The leaders set the example. Kouame, Sako and Liboko lived in moderation. They ate little, sharing their rations with their men and helping everyone with the work of securing the city. There was no way out. The city was surrounded. The reserves were running out. But the people of Massaba behaved as if they were not thinking of this and as if they believed victory was still possible. The weeks passed. Their faces became gaunt, and no victory came. Every day the warriors of Massaba managed, at the cost of a new effort each time, to drive back the assailants. Since Danga's intrusion no one had succeeded in breaking down a door or taking a section of wall.

In the nomad camp the men were losing patience. Bandiagara and Orios in particular grumbled repeatedly about these walls that refused to fall. They urged Sango Kerim to repeat the strategy that had worked so well with Danga. Massaba's forces were too few to tolerate attacks over a longer front. They only need attack in two or three different places. Sango Kerim agreed. Everything was prepared for the umpteenth assault on Massaba. Bandiagara was to command the first attack. Danga led the second. And Orios and Sango Kerim were to strike in a deserted part of the wall.

Battle commenced once more. There were the cries of the injured, the bellows of men trying to bolster their own courage, calls for help, insults and the clash of weapons. Once again sweat formed beads on every brow. Oil rained down over bodies, and blistered corpses lay at the foot of the walls.

The Ashes hurled themselves at the Gate of the Owl like ogres. There were only fifty of them but nothing seemed able to resist them. They ripped open the bolted shafts holding up the gate and crushed the guards, who were astonished to find themselves confronted with such giants. For the second time the nomads penetrated Massaba, and for the second time panic spread through the streets of the city. The news flew from house to house. The Ashes were advancing, killing everyone in their path. When the news reached him, young Liboko rushed to the front line. A handful of men from Tsongor's special guard followed him. His face was illuminated with rage. They came across the troop of Ashes just as the latter invaded the Square of Moonlight, a little square where storytellers gathered to speak of great adventures and where, on summer nights, the sweet whisper of fountains could be heard. Liboko hurled himself at the enemy like a demon. He pierced bellies and cut off limbs. He drove his lance through chests and disfigured faces. Liboko was fighting on his own ground, defending his city, and it was as if the ardour that sustained him would never leave him. He struck out tirelessly, breaking through the enemy lines in all his fury. The enemy troops were flattened by the force of his charges. Suddenly he raised his arm. A man was at his feet. There, at his mercy. He could cave in his skull, but he did not. He stayed there thus, with his arm raised, for an infinite moment. He had recognized his enemy. It was Sango Kerim. Their eyes met. Liboko looked upon the face of this man who, for so long, had been his friend. He could not bring himself to strike him. He smiled gently. It was at this moment that Orios launched himself. He had watched the entire scene. He could see that Sango Kerim might be killed at any moment. He did not hesitate and with the full weight of his mace he crushed Liboko's face. His body slumped to the ground. Life had already left him. A powerful groan of satisfaction escaped from Orios's bosom. Sango Kerim fell to his knees, devastated. He dropped his weapons, took off his helmet and took in his arms the body of this man who had not wanted to kill him. His face was a crater of flesh. And it was in vain that Sango Kerim scanned it for the gaze that had met his eyes just a few moments earlier. He wept over Liboko as the battle raged around him. The special guard had watched the scene and a profound fury roused them. They drove back the Ashes with all their might. They wanted to recover the body of their leader, that he might not be abandoned to the enemy. They wanted to bury him with his weapons beside his father. Orios was forced to retreat in the face of their violent onslaught. His men abandoned the body. They abandoned the Square of Moonlight. They took with them Sango Kerim who had no strength left, and they went back out through the city walls to escape the men of the special guard who pursued them, bellowing.

News of Liboko's death descended on Massaba and the nomad camp at the same time. Sango Kerim ordered his troops to withdraw. This day, for him, was accursed and no more blows should be struck. They climbed back up to the encampment, slowly, without speaking, like a vanquished army, heads lowered, while within Massaba the shrill cries of the weeping women began to ring out. Moaning could be heard from every direction. The city wept for one of its children. Sango Kerim sent Rassamilagh to tell Sako he could bury his brother in peace. The nomad warriors would not leave their hilltop camp. Ten days of mourning were decreed. The war, once again, was suspended. Liboko's body was cleaned and clothed. He was buried in the palace crypt with his weapons. And for ten days the hired mourners took turns beside the tomb to quench the dead man's thirst with the tears of the living.

IN THE HALL OF THE catafalque, King Tsongor had risen. His body, the emaciated old body of a dead man, was so thin that in places it seemed to be transparent. Katabolonga looked upon his king in astonishment. He thought that Tsongor was returning from the dead. Then he saw the king's face and he understood that it was his pain, a very acute pain, that had caused him to rise in this manner. He stood there, mouth agape, making no sound. He moved his hand as if to point towards something he could not name. Katabolonga lowered his eyes.

'What do you want of me, Tsongor?'

The king gave no reply and came closer to his friend. His deathly rigidity made his features unbearable to behold. Katabolonga spoke again.

'You have seen him, have you not? Did you see your son pass before you? You threw yourself at his feet but your arms could take hold of nothing. Or perhaps you simply stood there frozen? Unable to take one step towards him. You looked on Liboko's gentle smile. That is so, is it not? Yes, I know. What do you want of me, Tsongor?'

Silence, once again, filled the underground hall.

Katabolonga looked upon his friend's staring eyes. His lips quivered gently. Katabolonga strained his ears. A distant sound reached him. He concentrated. King Tsongor was speaking very quietly. The same chant repeated over and over again. Katabolonga listened. Yes. It was that. The same infinitely repeated words came from the dead man's lips with increasing force, until they filled the entire hall. The same three words. And all the corpse could do was to repeat them as he stared at Katabolonga.

'Return it now . . . return it now . . . return it now . . .'

Katabolonga did not understand. He thought Tsongor was speaking of Liboko. He was overcome with sorrow. He would have liked to weep.

'You know that if I could, I would give you back your son,' he said. 'But I myself spread the shroud over his body. There is nothing I can do.'

Tsongor interrupted him. His voice was stronger now, more assured.

'The coin . . . return it now . . .'

He was speaking now as he had in days gone by. But it was no longer the gentle murmur of a voice enjoying the meanderings of a conversation. It was a hoarse voice used to giving orders.

'The coin I gave you, Katabolonga. Return it now. I cannot go any further. It is over. I saw him. Yes. With a smile on his lips. Half his face crushed. Our eyes met. He did not stop. His smile slid over me. The coin I gave you, Katabolonga, it is time you returned it. Place it between my teeth and ensure the dead jaws are clamped tight that it should not fall. I am leaving. I cannot look upon this. No. They shall all pass through. One by one. For many years. Liboko is the first. I shall be a spectator to the slow bleeding away of those dear to me. Return it now, that I may rest in peace.'

Katabolonga had remained seated before his sovereign's corpse, with his head lowered. When Tsongor had finished, he rose slowly to his feet and unfurled himself to his full height, the full height of a living man. They were face to face once again, as they had been on that distant day when the last survivor of the Men who Crawl had defied the conqueror. Katabolonga did not tremble. He looked the king in the eye, unblinking.

'I shall give you nothing, Tsongor. You yourself wished for this suffering to which you are condemned. I shall give you nothing. You made me swear. You know that Katabolonga does not go back on his word.'

They stayed there for a long time, face to face. The pain within Tsongor sketched horrifying grimaces across his face. It was as if his mouth longed to capture all the air in that vaulted hall. Then, once again, an inaudible murmuring emanated from the depths of his body. He turned his back on Katabolonga, returned to his tomb and resumed his deathly stillness. Only this frail supplication continued to sound from his emaciated body.

'Return it now . . . return it now . . .'

For three whole days Tsongor whispered in the dense silence of the underground hall. Katabolonga squeezed his hand with all his strength, that Tsongor might feel his presence in the depths of his death. That he might not doubt his loyalty. But he did not return the rusted coin. He waited, crushed by his sorrow, for the chant to run dry and for the dead man to resume his silence.

FOR TEN DAYS SAMILIA STOOD on the crest of the hill. She looked down upon the city. She let the sounds of the city rise up to her, the mutterings of the weeping crowds and the slow ceremonial music. She no longer spoke to anyone. Since the day she had insulted Danga, she lived in the refuge of her tent. She now had confirmation of what she had always known. Misfortune lay heavy upon her, and it would never leave her now.

That is what Sango Kerim gradually came to understand too, and he confided in his friend Rassamilagh:

'Tomorrow the fighting will begin again and I say to you, Rassamilagh, a strange fear has blossomed within me. Not the fear of dying or of being vanquished. No. Those are fears we all know. The fear that we might once again penetrate Massaba. For each time our troops have entered the city it has brought me only pain and consternation. First the fire which consumed the towers of my childhood. Then the death of Liboko.'

Rassamilagh listened to him and answered:

'I understand your fear, Sango Kerim. It is sound. There shall be no victory.'

And he was right. Sango Kerim understood him. He looked upon the city at his feet as it prepared for battle the following day, and he knew that the siege of Massaba was madness. Over the days, months and years to come he would know only the alternating rhythm of victories and periods of mourning. And even the victories would have a deep-seated taste of injury for they would be won over men and over a city that he loved.

In Saramine Souba began work on the first of Tsongor's tombs. Shalamar opened the doors of her palace to him. She offered him her gold, her greatest architects and her master craftsmen. It was not long before the city reverberated with the constant activity of the stonemasons.

It was in the hanging gardens of Saramine that Souba decided to build the tomb. It was the highest point of the citadel. The gardens spread through a luxuriant succession of terraces and flights of steps. The fruit trees provided shade for the fountains. The view encompassed the entire city, the tall silhouettes of the towers and the motionless sea. Souba had the largest of the terraces altered so that a palace could be erected there. He wanted it to be of the local white stone. It took months on end of arduous work for the outline of the tomb to emerge. The exterior was pure and dazzling. In the halls within, tall statues reigned impassively over the marble flags on the floor.

When the work was at last finished, Souba invited Shalamar to visit the tomb before he sealed the door. They walked through it together, in silence. Wandering through the vast rooms, gazing upon the detailed mosaics on the ground, or the splendour of the views from the

balconies. Shalamar, a small silhouette full of wonder-
ment, frequently stopped to caress the stone columns
with the flat of her hand. When, at last, they came out,
she turned to Souba and said:

'What you have built here, Souba, is the tomb of
Tsongor the glorious. I thank you for giving to Saramine
a palace of such magnitude. From this day it will be the
silent heart of the city, a place where no one sets foot,
but venerated by everyone.'

It was then that Souba understood. He understood that
what he must do was create a portrait of his father. Seven
tombs to reflect the seven faces of Tsongor. The one in
Saramine was the face of the king crowned in glory, of the
man with an exceptional destiny who had spoken on equal
terms with the very light of the sun for all of his life. All
that remained for Souba to do was to present the various
different faces of Tsongor. One tomb for each of them, in
the four corners of the kingdom. And the seven tombs
together would express who Tsongor had been. This is
what remained for him to do. To find the place and the
form that each of his other faces was to take.

One last time he spent the sea-swept night of Saramine
beside Shalamar and, in the morning, he bid his farewells
and climbed back onto his mule. He left the black sail
of the washerwomen of Massaba in the ageing sovereign's palace. She had tied it to the highest tower in the

citadel. He had a whole continent yet to cover. The entire
kingdom now knew that Souba was abroad, looking here
and there for a place in which to build a funeral palace.
It was an honour to which every city, every region aspired.

Astride his obstinate mule, he travelled the kingdom
as an architect. In the Forest of the Screaming Baobabs
he had a tall pyramid constructed, a tomb for Tsongor
the great builder, amid the thick humus and the shrieks
of birds with flaming red plumage. Then he went to the
furthermost point of the kingdom, in the Archipelago of
Mangroves. These were the last lands before oblivion,
the last lands in which the name Tsongor made men fall
to their knees. There he built an island cemetery for
Tsongor the explorer, he who had pushed back the limits
of this earth, who had gone further than the most am-
bitious of men. For Tsongor the warrior, leader of armies
and military strategist, he carved two vast troglodyte halls
into the high rocky plateau of the Middle Lands. There,
deep below ground, he ordered the craftsmen to create
thousands of statuettes of warriors, large mannequins of
clay, each of them different. He distributed them through
the dark, underground caverns, a vast army of stone
soldiers carpeting the floor, like a nation of petrified
warriors, ready to swing into action at any moment.

Waiting patiently for their king's return in order to march once again. When he had finished the tomb of the warrior, Souba looked for a place where he might build a tomb for Tsongor the father, the man who had raised five children lovingly and with generosity. In the Desert of the Solitary Fig Trees, among the lizards and the wind-swept dunes, he erected a tall tower of ochre stone which could be seen several days' march away. At the top of the tower he set a stone from the swamps, a great translucent block which irradiated through the night all the light it had accumulated during the day. The stone fed off the desert sun and illuminated the night like a lighthouse for nomadic caravans.

The eternal face of Tsongor was gradually being constructed through Souba's sweat and self-effacement as he abandoned himself to his task. The tombs sprang up and it seemed to him, every time he completed one of their number, every time he sealed the door of one of these silent resting places and left the site, it seemed to him that he heard a distant sigh upon his shoulder. He knew what this meant. Tsongor was there, beside him. Through his nights of dreaming and his days of toil, Tsongor was there. And this sigh that Souba heard with each completed tomb always told him the same thing. That he had acquitted himself of his task and Tsongor was thanking him. Yes, with each new tomb Tsongor was thanking him. But each sigh also told him that this was not yet the one, and that the place was still to be found. So, tireless, Souba set off again. Looking, once more, for a place that would be fitting. That he might feel at last upon his shoulder his father's sigh of relief.

Chapter V

SHE WHO WAS
FORGOTTEN

MASSABA STILL HELD FIRM, BUT its appearance had changed. The city that now dominated the plain was drained of its blood. The walls looked as if they might implode at any moment. The reserves of food and water were all but exhausted. Hordes of vultures circled above the walls and dived onto bodies that had not been burned. The city was filthy and its inhabitants exhausted. The warriors' faces were gaunt, like those of ageing horses, lost in the desert, stumbling on stubbornly towards the horizon until finally their strength leaves them and they collapse in the warm sands of death. No one spoke any more. Everyone was waiting, resigned, for life to stop.

In Tsongor's palace everything had been defiled. One entire wing had been ravaged by the fire. No one had had either the time or the energy to restore it. It was a heap of burned carpets, fallen ceilings and blackened walls. The corridors had aged and grown dirty. Whole rooms, which had once served as reception halls, were now dormitories accumulating weary bodies. The great terrace of the palace had been converted into a hospital.

The injured were tended there, overlooking the fighting below the city walls. The strength of the whole structure was ebbing away. It could collapse at any moment. The roads were now no more than tracks of beaten earth. The cobblestones had been used to throw at the enemy. The gardens had been ransacked to feed the horses. Then, later, with hunger threatening, the animals had been killed to feed the people.

Since his brother's death, Sako was completely transformed. He had become so thin that the long necklaces he wore over his chest made a dry rattling sound as they knocked against his ribs. He had allowed his beard to grow long, and this, at certain times, made him look like his father's corpse. Massaba's army had been decimated. Of the forces that had once been gathered, there remained little more than the special guard and Gonomor's Fern Peoples. Alongside Kouame there were now only Arkalas and Barnak with his Khat Grinders. That was all. A handful of men, exhausted by months of uninterrupted fighting.

Kouame sensed that defeat was upon them. He would fall there, with Massaba, amid his assailants' cries of joy.

So one night, without speaking a word to anyone, he took off his armour, put on a long dark tunic and left the city. It was a heavy night, the air too dense to bear a scent. He slipped like a shadow across the great plain which had been the site of so many battles, and climbed up towards the hills. Once there, he stole through the encampment armed only with a dagger. He passed straight through the men and their animals with a determined step, and no one stopped him for he looked so like one of Rassamilagh's veiled warriors. He waited a little longer for the camp to go to sleep, then gently, without making a sound, he entered Samilia's tent.

He found Tsongor's daughter lying upon her bed patiently taking out the dozens of clasps that held her hair.

'Who are you?' she asked with a start.

'Kouame, Prince of the Lands of Salt,' he replied.

'Kouame?'

She was on her feet, wide-eyed and trembling. He took a step forward into the tent so as not to risk being seen from outside, and removed the veils that concealed his face.

'It is no surprise to me that you do not recognize me, Samilia, for I am not the same man I once was.'

There was silence for a time. Kouame thought Samilia might ask him another question, but she did not. She could not, so paralysed was she by her surprise.

'Do not tremble, Samilia. I am at your mercy,' he went on. 'You need but call out and I would be in your men's hands. Do as you wish. It matters little to me. I shall be dead tomorrow.'

She did not call out. She looked upon the grimacing features before her, but could not recognize the man she had once seen. The wide, round, confident face of the past had become hollow and lined. It was now dry and angular, and seemed to be in the clutches of a fever. Only the look in his eyes was the same. Yes, those eyes that had met hers at the foot of Tsongor's catafalque. Those eyes that saw everything of her.

'You know it is so, do you not?' he continued. 'They must have told you. We are slowly dying in Massaba. Tomorrow it will surely come to an end. And it will be on the points of spears that you will see our heads march past in a long procession. That is why I am here.'

'What do you want?' she asked.

'You know very well, Samilia. Look at me. You know, do you not?'

She had indeed known the very moment their eyes had met. He had come for her. Through the enemy tents, stealing between them to this place to possess her. She knew this, and it seemed obvious to her that it should be thus. Yes. He had come to her, the day before he was to die, and she knew that what he wished for, she would grant him. Her desire had never left her. Since that day when she had seen him for the first time, and in spite of the choice she had made to join Sango Kerim, something urged her to yield to Kouame. She had chosen Sango Kerim out of duty, to remain faithful to her past. But when she saw him, she knew that she belonged to Kouame. In spite of herself, in spite of the war which would never allow their union, it was so. She did not move. He stepped closer to her. She could feel his breath on her breast.

'I shall die tomorrow. But that matters little to me if before then I shall know the taste of you.'

She closed her eyes and felt Kouame's hand removing her clothes. They dropped down onto the bed and he took her, there, in the sweat of that windless night, amid the voices of the enemy camp, the comings and goings of soldiers and the crackle of the watch fires. He took her and she streamed with pleasure for the first time. She opened all of herself wide, biting into the cushions to avoid the risk of screaming out loud. All along her thighs the long moist quivers succeeded each other, quenching Kouame's thirst as he stayed over her, his head buried in her hair. He washed his soul of the injuries of war. He intoxicated himself, one last time, on the smell of life. The tent filled with the heavy scent of their embraces, and every time he made as if to leave she clasped him once again into the innermost depths of her body, and he slipped forward pleasurably, his head swimming with the sweetness of her.

Before the sun rose, Kouame left Samilia's bed to steal back through the enemy camp and return to the city. Samilia stroked his face. He accepted her caress. This hand on his cheek was bidding him adieu. It said simply: 'Go. Now it is time to die.'

When he had gone, she remained motionless for a long time. Since she had adopted Sango Kerim's camp something within her had been dead. She had chosen to be there, among these men who fought for her; chosen to be there, but emptied of passion. Simply awaiting the outcome of the war, that there might be no more suffering and that life might start again. Kouame's visit had overturned everything.

'I did not know how to choose,' she thought. 'Or I made the wrong choice. I chose the past and obedience. I silenced the desire within me. I joined Sango Kerim out of loyalty. But life demanded that I choose Kouame. No, it could not be so. Had I chosen Kouame, I would now be weeping for Sango Kerim. But it could not be so. There is no possible choice. I belong to two men. Yes, I belong to them both. That is my punishment.

There shall be no happiness for me. I belong to them both. A fevered, divisive existence. That is it. That is all that I am. A woman of war. In spite of myself. A woman of war who begets only hatred and fighting.'

When Kouame came before Samilia he had accepted death. The battles of the last few months had slowly worn him down. Defeat seemed certain. All around him he could see only exhaustion and resignation. He had set out to find Samilia as a condemned man requests one last favour. Tasting of this woman was the only way of leaving this life with no regrets. He wanted to caress her before the massacre. To know the smell of her. To be pervaded by it. And still to smell her on his body in that moment when he put his knee to the ground. He thought that once he had held Samilia in his arms he would be ready to die. But the truth was exactly the opposite. Since his return to Massaba a black rage boiled within him. His whole body, although exhausted and grown so thin, was racked by a brusque nervous energy. He muttered to himself, constantly cursing himself.

'Yesterday I was ready to die. I was calm. They were free to come. I was not afraid of anything any more. I would have had a fitting death, without sparing a glance for my enemies. And now . . . now I am to die, yes, but it will be with regret. She covered me with kisses. She clasped me between her thighs; her belly was soft. And

I have to take my place again along the walls. No. I now know what I am losing, and it would have been better had I not known.'

He was the only man along the walls who showed the slightest movement. All the others were quite motionless, in a haze of weariness, like children woken in the dead of night and put on their feet, who stay just where they have been put, dazed. They were ready to die. They wanted nothing other than this death which would relieve them of their exhaustion. Kouame spat on the ground, bellowed and drove his fist against the fortified wall, crying: 'Let them come, let them come and be done with it!' He did not take his eyes off the hills where the encampment was and where, at the very moment that the nomad army set off at a march, he thought he could see a tiny, motionless point watching him. 'Samilia,' he thought. 'She has come to see whether we shall die a fitting death.'

On that day, once again, the warriors threw themselves fiercely at the ramparts. But as the first of them reached the fortifications, a strange noise could be heard in the distance. An army was marching down the hill to the south, an army that could not yet be identified. 'This now is truly the end,' thought Kouame. 'The sons of she-dogs have more reinforcements.' From the top of the walls they watched the great cloud of dust raised by this unknown army with all the feeble curiosity of a condemned man looking on his executioner's hood. They wanted to know who it was that would massacre them. But they saw the nomad army rapidly withdrawing and assuming a defensive position. And the more they looked, the more clearly they saw that it was indeed towards their enemies that the reinforcements were charging. Their outlines were now becoming clearer.

'But . . . they are women,' murmured Sako, his mouth open with amazement.

'Women,' confirmed old Barnak.

'Mazehbu,' Kouame whispered.

He repeated the name more and more loudly. 'Mazehbu, Mazehbu.' His men all along the wall heard the word and called it out, without understanding its meaning, like a war cry, a cry of relief to thank the gods. Mazehbu. Mazehbu. And to each of them this strange word meant: 'We shall perhaps not die this day.'

'But who is it?' Sako asked Kouame.

The Prince of the Lands of Salt replied: 'My mother.'

It was indeed the Empress Mazehbu marching down the hillside at the head of her army. She was given this name because she was the mother of her people, and she and her Amazons rode zehbus with their long, straight, pointed horns. She was a huge woman, covered in diamonds, and of all the political minds in her kingdom she had the sharpest. She excelled in court intrigues and commercial negotiations. But every time her kingdom declared war, she herself stood at the head of the army and metamorphosed into a wild beast. She constantly hurled unspeakable insults at her enemies, and in combat she knew neither leniency nor compassion. Her army was made up only of Amazons who had learned the art of combat at a full gallop. They wielded their bows and arrows as they rode, and to facilitate their skill they had each had their right breast removed.

The nomad army was gripped with amazement. They had become so accustomed to the daily rhythm of their attacks on the city, they were so convinced that Massaba would now soon fall, that, faced with this unexpected charge carried out by an army they did not know, they quite simply knew not what to do. Caught in the very middle of the plain in that way, and cut off from their camp, they felt infinitely vulnerable. When they were able to identify Mazehbu's Amazons, when they saw this army of brightly painted women mounted on zehbus, they thought this must be some form of macabre joke. Soon Mazehbu's foul-mouthed shrieking carried to them. She was shrieking with all her might as she spurred on her mount.

'Come here that I might crush your nose and see you roll in the dust. Come here, mongrels. This is the end of your good fortune. Come. Mazehbu is here to punish you . . .'

A skyful of arrows rained down on the first of the nomad warriors. The Amazons kept firing as they advanced. The closer they came, the truer and more murderous was their every shot. When the impact between the two armies came, the zehbus ran their long, sharpened horns through countless warriors. Sango Kerim knew that if they remained on the plain, his army would be decimated. As he called a retreat to the encampment, they were routed. The Amazons did not launch themselves in pursuit. They lined up one beside the other and, with perfect calm and concentration, loosed their arrows, which plucked off the nomads in their flight. They fell as one, mown down as they ran, falling face down in the earth. The Amazons' bows, crafted from the supple wood of the sequoia tree, fired further than any other bow. The nomads had to cross the entire plain before they were free of danger.

* * *

For the first time in months, on that day Massaba did not have to fight along its fortified walls. For the first time in months Massaba's armies could leave the city and take up positions on three of the seven hills. The siege of Massaba came to an end. And the whole city blessed the strange name they now heard for the first time: Mazehbu.

For the whole of the rest of the day, and on into the night, the city was consumed with frenetic activity. The dead were removed from the pyres that had been improvised on all the squares. Ditches were dug outside the walls and the dead were buried that the city might no longer risk disease. Groups of warriors hurried out onto the plain to reclaim weapons, helmets and armour from the nomads killed by the Amazons. Grass and wheat were fetched to feed the livestock and the people themselves. The makeshift hospital was transferred to the palace cellars, which were cooler, better protected and easier to reach. And finally, when the moon was already high in the sky, an enormous banquet was organized on the terrace of Massaba. It was as if the entire city were heaving a great sigh of relief. Mazehbu had pride of place, dominating the gathering amid an intermingling of warriors and Amazons. She wanted to know the name of each one of them, to enquire after their least wound. Then, when at last Mazehbu and her son found themselves alone together for a moment, she took his hand, looked upon him at length and said:

'You have grown thin, my son.'

'We have been under siege for many months, mother,' he replied.

'You have aged too,' she said.

'We have not ceased causing death and having death brought on us,' he replied.

'This is the mark of Samilia that I see in your face. I look at you and I know her. She has lined your face. It is good that it should be so.'

She said nothing more. She invited her son to drink and together they celebrated this day, which had not seen the downfall of Massaba.

SOUBA CONTINUED TO FOLLOW HIS path across the
kingdom. This time spent roaming the land, which had
at first frightened him, was something he learned to
love. He was no longer eager to reach some town or
to find the site of another tomb. He travelled along the
roadways, moving from one place to another to the
complete indifference of the world, and this indifference did him good. He no longer had a name or a past.
He lived in silence. To those who came across him he
was merely a traveller. New lands unfurled before him.
He succumbed to the soothing rhythm of his mule's
steady footfalls, happy to have nothing else to do, in
those moments, than to contemplate the world and let
the light inhabit him.

Slowly, he made his way to Solanos, the city on the
river Tanak. The river crossed a great desert, and when
it eventually threw itself into the sea the landscape
suddenly changed. The banks were covered in date palms,
like an oasis in the middle of this barren, stony ground.
It was here that Solanos had been built. It was the site

of one of his father's most famous battles. It was said that King Tsongor's army had crossed the desert to launch a surprise attack on the people of Solanos, who had expected the conquerors to arrive downstream. They had suffered the burning of the intractable sun, which made the very rocks split and crack. Exhausted by the hardships, they had even been forced to eat their horses. Some of them had gone mad. Others had been blinded for life. With every day that passed Tsongor's columns of marching men grew smaller. When they arrived at Solanos they were drained of all their strength. Legend has it that Solanos then witnessed Tsongor's anger. This was not so. It was not anger which caused the king's men to throw themselves on the city with such frenzied ferocity. It was the desert, their stupor and their madness. The days in the desert had destroyed their minds, and they threw themselves savagely upon Solanos. Soon there was nothing left of the city.

Souba wanted to reach this place, to see these walls about which he had heard so much during his childhood. He rode along the river with its slow, dense waters. When he reached Solanos and came before the wise men of the city, he could sense great agitation around him, a strange agitation which he himself had not caused. Something had happened to make the very paving-stones in the streets hum. He gave his name and was greeted with all the respect owed to his standing. He was offered rooms and a meal but, despite this consideration, Souba still felt that his arrival had been eclipsed by some other event. This aroused his curiosity.

'What is happening?' he asked his host. 'Why is your city so agitated?'

'He has returned,' his host replied fearfully.

'Who?' asked Souba.

'Galash. The horseman of the river. He has returned. It is decades now since he has been seen. He was believed dead, but he was there this morning. Out of nowhere, he was there once again. As he used to be.'

Souba listened. He wanted to know more. Calmly, he invited his host to sit down beside him, to drink with him and to tell him who this horseman was, whose return was so strange. The host accepted his invitation and told him what he knew.

It was in the days of the siege of Solanos. It was said that on the very evening of the victory, a soldier came forward from the ranks and asked to speak to the king. Tsongor was celebrating the destruction of the city, surrounded by his personal guard amid the mingling smell of ashes and date palms. The soldier came before him. His name was Galash. No one knew him. He looked like a madman, but Tsongor was not troubled. All of his army looked like this, with their eyes straining out of their sockets, after crossing the desert and the furious fighting that had ensued. Each of his men had been gripped by the same madness. Each had known the pleasure of destruction. The soldier came before the king, and Tsongor thought at first that he wanted to ask some favour of him. But it was not so.

'I asked to see you, Tsongor, for what I have to say I wish to say directly to you. I believed in you for a long time. In your strength. In your military genius. In the strength of your leadership. I followed you from the first day, and I asked for nothing, neither promotion nor favour. I was one of your soldiers, and that was sufficient for me. One among so many. But today, Tsongor, today I have come before you to curse you. I spit on your name, your throne and your power. I crossed the desert with you. I watched my friends fall one by one, with their faces in the sand, and you did not deign to turn and look upon even one of them. I myself held out, thinking you would reward us for our loyalty and endurance. You gave us a city, yes. A massacre. That was your gift, Tsongor. And I spit on you. You unleashed us on Solanos like a pack of crazed dogs. You knew that we were drained of all our strength, intoxicated and deranged. That is what you wanted. You unleashed us on Solanos and we ripped the city apart like monsters. You know that. You were among us. That is what you made us, monsters whose hands will for ever bear the thick smell of blood. I curse you, Tsongor, for what you made of me. What I have just said, I shall continue to say from now on, everywhere that I go in the kingdom, to every person I meet. I shall leave you, Tsongor. I now know who you are.'

Thus spoke the soldier Galash. He was about to leave when Tsongor ordered that he be caught and forced to kneel before him. His lips were quivering with rage. He had risen from his throne.

'You shall go nowhere, soldier,' he replied, 'nowhere, for everything around you is mine. You are on my land. I could kill you for saying what you have said. I could tear out your tongue for insulting me before my men. But that is not what I shall do, out of respect for your loyalty through all these years of fighting. That is not what I shall do. You are wrong. I know how to thank my men. Your life is safe. But never set foot in a land of mine again. If you stay in my kingdom I shall order that you be torn limb from limb. Only the unexplored world is left to you, the wild lands where no man lives. Cross the river Tanak and live what years remain to you on the opposite bank.'

It was done according to Tsongor's wishes. That very

evening the soldier Galash crossed the great river and disappeared into the night. But the following morning he re-
appeared. There, on the opposite bank. His silhouette was
perfectly visible, mounted on his foaming horse. He
bellowed from the other side of the river. He bellowed
with all his strength that he might tell everyone what he
had to say about Tsongor. That the soldiers and the city's
inhabitants might hear him. He cursed the king at the top
of his lungs, but the sounds of the river covered his voice.
All that could be heard was a deep whispering of water.
He stayed thus for many months, coming back every day,
straining to shout above the roar of the river. Every day
with the same anger, like a mad horseman haranguing their
minds. Then one day, at last, he disappeared. No one saw
him again. Years passed. He was believed dead.

The day Souba arrived in Solanos Galash had reap-
peared for the first time in years, as if he had emerged
from the past. There was Galash, once again. Still on his
horse. Terribly aged. The anger that drove him appar-
ently intact. The horseman of the river had returned the
very day King Tsongor's son had set foot on the lands
of Solanos.

Souba listened to the story with curiosity. He had
never heard tell of this man. He felt, without really know-

ing why, that he should go to meet him. It seemed to him that Galash was doing only one thing: calling him.

With the first glow of dawn light Souba climbed onto his mule and made for the river. He saw Galash as he had been described to him – a shadow on horseback, riding up and down the opposite bank, gesticulating like a madman. He spurred his mule's flanks and rode into the waters of the river. As he made his way across the river he saw the silhouette of the horseman grow larger. He could see him quite clearly now but could still hear nothing. He urged his mule on again. At last the animal found its footing on the far side. Galash was there. Souba was stupefied by what he saw. The man before him was scraggy and very old. Naked to the waist and with his face and flanks withered with age, he looked like a demon. He was thin. Hunched. His haunted eyes rolled in their sockets. Souba gazed at him at length, watching this creature broken by the passage of time. What stupefied Souba was that he heard nothing. Galash had resumed his sweeping gestures and imprecations. His eyes, now harsh, still rolled in their sockets. But from his mouth not a sound came. He filled his lungs. The veins in his neck could be seen thickening. But Souba could hear only the thin thread of a broken voice. It was not the sound of the river that covered Galash's voice. For all these years he had been shouting with all his strength, until his very vocal cords had torn. He had spent decades shouting himself hoarse with rage. Now he produced only a distant, guttural sound. But Souba gradually forgot the strange sounds and looked on the horseman's face. And what he could not understand from the voice, he read in the face of this damned creature. There the deep lines spoke of the endless years of exile. The way in which he twisted his lips, the expressions that flitted over his face, they were all a translation of his sufferings and fears, the solitude and the loneliness. Galash wept and wrung his hands. Made flailing movements. Erupted with violent noises and tore at his forearms with his teeth.

They stood there for a long time, facing each other, taming each other. Then, with a tilt of his head, Galash invited Souba to follow him. He spurred on his horse and turned towards a track which led away from the banks of the river. Tsongor's son did not hesitate. So began the silent march along the pathways of the unexplored lands. The two animals progressed at a walk along the rocky track. They climbed the crest of a hillside. After several hours' journey the horseman stopped at last. They had reached the top of a mound overlooking the sea. Below them there was an inlet, a natural semi-circle. A putrid smell assailed Souba's nose. At his feet, over a vast expanse, a horrible spectacle was being played out. Thousands of giant turtles wallowed in nauseous sands. Some of them were dead, some dying. Others continued to struggle free. There was a great accumulation of empty shells and putrefying flesh. The air was polluted with the stench. Vultures flew back and forth, piercing the shells with their honed beaks. The spectacle was unbearable. The turtles were forced into the inlet by underground currents. They ran aground here, on this deadly beach which offered neither shelter nor food, without the strength to confront the currents once more to escape, and the vultures, in all their voracity, swooped down upon them. It was a vast animal cemetery, a trap laid by nature against which the great marine reptiles could do nothing. They kept coming, and the sand had disappeared beneath the dried bones and shells. Souba brought his hand to his mouth that he might avoid inhaling the stench of death that rose up to him. Galash no longer tried to speak. He no longer growled. He seemed appeased. Souba watched the slow, regular sway of the waves, and the vain attempts of the giant turtles to break away from the current. The vultures circled, intractable. He watched the slow ebb and flow of the sea, the movement of death. There was in this spectacle something absurd and appalling, like a huge, pointless carnage. Galash had brought him all the way here, and Souba understood why. A tomb must be built here, in this putrid place where these great reptiles imprisoned by the waters had been coming to groan in agony for so many years. A tomb for Tsongor the killer. Tsongor who had brought about the death of so many men, Tsongor who had razed cities and burned entire countries. A tomb for Tsongor the wild who knew no fear of blood, a tomb which would be his face of war. It was here that the sixth tomb must be built. For the portrait of Tsongor to be complete, there must be a grimace of horror. An accursed tomb, among the bones and the vultures replete with flesh.

WITH MAZEHBU'S ARRIVAL THERE WAS war once again. Once again the plain of Massaba was gorged with blood. The days and months passed to the rhythm of warriors advancing and retreating. Positions were taken, then lost, then taken again. Thousands of footsteps carved out pathways of suffering in the dust of the plain. They advanced. They retreated. They died. The bodies dried in the sun, were reduced to skeletons. Then the bones, bleached by time, crumbled, and more warriors came to die in these heaps of man-dust. It was the greatest slaughter the continent had ever known. Men aged. They grew thin, and war lent them all the grainy complexion of marble statues. But, despite the blows and the exhaustion, their vigour was undiminished and they continued to throw themselves at each other with the same fury, like two starved dogs driven mad by the sight of blood, who can think only of biting without realizing they are slowly dying.

One evening Mazehbu called for her son on the terrace of Massaba. It was hot. She stood very upright, sure of herself, determined, and spoke to Kouame with authority.

'Listen to me, Kouame, and do not interrupt. It is a long time now since I came here. A long time in which I have done battle alongside you. A long time in which I have known, every day, anger and privation. When I came I saved Massaba by driving back that dog Sango Kerim. But since then each of my assaults has been in vain. I call you here to tell you this, Kouame. Today I shall stop. Tomorrow I shall leave for the Kingdom of Salt. It is not good to leave the country any longer without a leader to govern it. You having nothing to fear. I shall go alone. I shall leave my Amazons with you. I do not wish Massaba to fall because I am withdrawing. But listen to this, Kouame. Listen to what your mother has to say. You wanted this woman and you have fought for her. What you have not been able to obtain thus far, the future will not offer to you. If Samilia is not already yours, she never will be. It surely means the gods have decided to withhold her from both of you. You are of equal strength and equal wile. You exhaust each other, and only the war grows and expands. Abandon this fight, Kouame. There is no shame in that. Bury your dead and spit on this city which has cost you so much. Spit on Samilia with her face of ash. While you are here all that life is doing is trickling out of you. You are losing your years on the walls of Massaba. I have so many other things for you. Leave this woman to Sango Kerim or to whomsoever would have her. You can expect nothing of her but cries and blood on the sheets. I see the way you look at me and I know what you think. No, I am not afraid of Sango Kerim. No, I am not fleeing the fighting. I came here to try to cleanse you of an insult. Whoever does that is not a coward. But there is no glory in leading men to their deaths. Resign yourself to this, Kouame. Come with me. We shall offer Sako and his men hospitality in our kingdom that they may not have their throats cut here after we have left. We shall all leave Massaba, by night, without a word. And in the morning it will be a dead city that those dogs finally take into their possession, and, believe me, you will hear no cries of joy in the distance. For at the very moment that they step into the gloomy, lifeless streets of Massaba they will understand that there is no victory. They will even understand, as they grit their teeth with fury, that we have left the war in order to embrace life, and that we have left them there, in the dusts of war, to live with death and their fruitless dreams.'

Thus spoke Mazehbu. Kouame listened to her without a word, his face inscrutable. He did not take his eyes off her. When she had finished he said simply:

'You gave me life twice, my mother. The day you were

delivered of me, and the day you came to save Massaba. You have nothing to be ashamed of. Glory goes before you. Go home to our kingdom in peace, but do not ask me to follow you. There is still, for me, a woman who must be taken and a man who must be killed.'

The Empress Mazehbu left Massaba by night, on her royal zehbu, escorted by a dozen Amazons. She left behind her son dreaming of blood-soaked wedding celebrations. She left the seven hills shrouded in a slow death.

The war continued, and victory would not choose its camp. The two armies grew increasingly filthy and exhausted. In every direction there were pitiful, emaciated figures, bodies dried out and worn down by mourning and the passing years.

FOR SEVERAL NIGHTS NOW KING Tsongor's body had seemed tormented. It twitched and writhed like a child gripped by fever. In his deathly sleep, twisted grimaces flitted over his face. It was not unusual for Katabolonga to see him blocking his ears with his skeletal hands. The servant did not know what to do. Something was at play here, something he could not grasp. He could but watch the fearful progress of anxiety through the aged sovereign's body. One night, eventually, the exhausted Tsongor opened his eyes and began to speak. His voice had changed. It was the voice of the vanquished.

'My father's laughter has returned,' he said.

Of Tsongor's father Katabolonga knew nothing. He had never spoken of him. It had always seemed to him that Tsongor had been born of the union of a horse and a city. He remained silent and Tsongor went on:

'My father's laughter. I can hear it echoing through my mind at every moment, with the same intonations as on the last day I saw him. He was on his bed. I had been called to him and told that he would soon die. He had barely caught sight of me before he started laughing, a horrible, contemptuous laugh which shook the entire length of his weary aged body. He laughed with hatred. He laughed to insult me. I did not stay. I never saw him again. It was then that I decided I should expect nothing from him. His laugh told me that he would bequeath me nothing. He laughed at my hopes of inheritance. He was wrong. Had he bequeathed me his dark little strip of a kingdom, I would not have wanted it. I wanted more. I wanted to build an empire to make people forget his. To wipe away the laughter. Everything that I have done since that day, the campaigns, the forced marches, the conquests, the cities I built, all of that I did to keep me far from my father's laughter. But it has come back today. I can hear it in the darkness now as I heard it in days gone by. With the same savage cruelty. Do you know what this laughter tells me, Katabolonga? It tells me that I have handed nothing on to those I love. I built this city. You know that better than any man. You were by my side. It was built to last. What is left of it now? It is the curse of the House of Tsongor, Katabolonga. From father to son nothing passes but dust and contempt. I have failed. I wanted to have an empire to bequeath, that my children might expand it still further. But my father has returned. He is laughing. And he is right. He is laughing over the death of Liboko. He is laughing over the burning of Massaba. He is laughing. Everything is collapsing and dying around me. I was presumptuous. I know what I should have done. In order to pass on the essence of what I am to my children, I should have passed on my father's laughter. I should have gathered them all together, the day before my death, and ordered that Massaba be burned before their eyes, so that there should be nothing left. That is what I should have done. And I should have laughed while the city burned, as my father laughed in days gone by. On my death there would have been just a little heap of ashes to inherit. And a fierce appetite. They would all have needed to build, to recoup the happiness of the life they had known. I would have passed on to them the desire to do better than myself. I would have bequeathed them this appetite, which would have gripped their bellies. They would perhaps have loathed me, as I loathed the laughter of that aged man insulting me on his death bed. But we would have been drawn together in our hatred of fathers. They would have been my sons. What are they now? The laughter is right. I should have destroyed everything.'

Katabolonga did not speak. He did not know what to say. Massaba was destroyed, Liboko killed. Perhaps Tsongor was right. Perhaps he had succeeded in handing on to those he loved nothing but the savage violence of a war horse, a taste for flames and for blood. Tsongor had that in him. Katabolonga knew that better than any man.

'You speak the truth, Tsongor,' he replied gently to the king. 'You have failed. Your children are devouring your empire and will keep nothing of you. But I am here. And you bequeathed me to Souba.'

At first Tsongor did not understand. He could not see how Katabolonga could think that he had been offered to his son as an inheritance. But it gradually seemed to him, although he could not explain why, that it was so. Everything was to be destroyed. Everything. Only Katabolonga would be left, impassive among the ruins, holding within him Tsongor's entire inheritance. Katabolonga's loyalty as he waited for Souba with his stubborn, unwavering patience. Perhaps he had handed that on to Souba. Yes, even though his son did not know it. Katabolonga's calm loyalty. He closed his eyes. Yes, his friend must be right. For his father's laughter no longer echoed around inside his head.

No, victory would not come. Mazehbu had left Massaba, and Kouame began to think that she had been right. He would never win. He could not resolve to leave as his mother had advised him. This was not for fear of being called a coward. He cared nothing about that. But the thought that he would be leaving behind Sango Kerim to have the pleasure of Samilia appalled him. He imagined their future embraces, and it caused him to retch with disgust. And yet the desire to fight had left him. He had grown less ingenious. He mounted each charge with less fury. One evening, returning from a combat which, once again, had been a paltry mêlée from which no one had emerged the victor, he looked on his brothers-in-arms. Aged Barnak had bent over with the passage of time. He advanced into battle with his back hunched. His shoulder blades could be seen clearly through the skin. He spoke to himself, and nothing now could draw him out of his smoke-filled dreams. Arkalas, for his part, never removed his clothes of war. In his tent in the evenings he laughed at the ghosts around him. Sako was still vigorous but the beard that he had allowed to grow over all these years made him look like an ageing warrior hermit. Only Gonomor had perhaps not changed. But he was the priest of the gods, and on him time used gentler claws. Kouame looked on the gathering of his friends returning from the battlefield, dragging their weapons, their feet and their thoughts in the dust. He saw this troop of long-haired, bearded men who had long ceased to live or speak or laugh. He encompassed them with one glance and whispered:

'It is not possible. This must cease.'

In the morning he ordered that everyone should prepare to go down into the great plain of Massaba. He sent a messenger to Sango Kerim to tell him that he was waiting for him. He asked him to come with Samilia. He gave his word that today he would not attempt any trickery.

The two armies prepared as they had so many times before. But, as he put on his leather armour or saddled his horse, each man felt that something would happen today to alter the course of the massacre.

The two armies descended onto the plain to the slow rhythm of the horses' walk. The animals' hooves crushed skulls and other bones in their path. When the two armies stood facing each other, less than a hundred paces apart, they froze. They were all there. In the ranks of the nomads were Rassamilagh, Bandiagara, Orios, Danga and Sango Kerim. Facing them, in silence, stood Sako, Kouame, Gonomor, Barnak and Arkalas. Beside Sango Kerim was Samilia. She was mounted on a jet black horse. Her face was hidden beneath veils. She sat upright and impassive, still dressed in mourning.

Kouame then made his way forwards. When he was a few paces from Sango Kerim and Samilia, he spoke up clearly, that every man might hear what he had to say.

'It is strange, Sango Kerim, for me to find myself face to face with you once more,' he said. 'I shall not deny it. For a long time I believed your mother had been delivered of a corpse and I had but to knock you down to watch your bones flounder in the dust. But we have not ceased to do battle, and not one of my blows has succeeded in felling you. Once again I find myself face to face with you, almost within touching distance, and I want to throw myself at you, so close do you seem and so easy to kill. I would do so if I did not know that, once again, the gods would separate us without my wetting my lips with your blood. I hate you, Sango Kerim, let there be no doubt. But there is to be no victory for me, I know this.'

'You speak the truth, Kouame,' replied Sango Kerim.

'I would never have believed that I could stand so close to you without doing everything in my power to slit your throat. But I too have heard the gods whispering to me that I shall not know that joy. They will not offer it to me.'

'I look at your army, Sango Kerim,' Kouame went on, 'and I see, with some pleasure, that it is in the same state as mine. They are now two crowds worn down by their weariness, clinging to their lances that they might stay on their feet. Sango Kerim, we must acknowledge that we are at breaking point and that the only thing still flourishing on this plain is death.'

'You speak the truth, Kouame,' Sango Kerim said again. 'We march into war like sleepwalkers.'

'Here are my thoughts, Sango Kerim,' Kouame continued after a while. 'After so much fighting, neither of us would agree to give up Samilia. There would be too much shame in capitulation. There is only one solution.'

'I am listening,' said Sango Kerim.

'Samilia should do what her father did before her. She should take her own life. To seal the peace,' said Kouame.

There was a vast uproar in both armies, a great din of clinking bridles and men's voices. Sango Kerim stood pale and open-mouthed. He could but ask:

'What is it you are saying?'

'She will belong to no one,' Kouame repeated. 'You know it as well as I. We shall all die without claiming her. Samilia is the very face of ill-fortune. Let her cut her own throat, that throat on which no one shall ever lay a hand. Do not think that it is easy for me to condemn her thus. The longing to make her mine has never been stronger than it is today. But with Samilia's death our two armies could suspend the fighting and avoid death.'

Kouame had spoken with great spirit. His face was now flushed. It was clear that the words he had just uttered had scorched him. He twisted awkwardly in the saddle.

'How do you dare speak thus?' replied Sango Kerim. 'I believed, for a moment, that you were in possession of your senses, but I see that these years of fighting have made you lose your mind.'

Kouame looked exultant. Not so much because of what Sango Kerim had said. He had scarcely heard. No. Because of the raging passion that boiled within him. What he had said, he had not wanted to say. He saw Samilia, impassive, before him, and he was condemning her to death when he wanted to take her in his arms. But he had spoken, feverishly. And now he had to see this through to the end, even if it meant being driven mad by the pain.

'Do not put on that air of outrage, Sango Kerim,'

Kouame went on. 'You defend this woman. That proves your honour. But what I have to tell you will change your opinion. She gave herself to me, this woman that you cherish. Even when she had chosen your camp, she abandoned her body to me, one night, in the encampment. I am not lying. She is there. She can tell you. Is it true, Samilia?'

There was perfect silence. Even the vultures stopped picking over the scraps of flesh on the corpses and turned their heads towards the gathering of warriors. Samilia sat impassive. With her face still hidden beneath her veils, she said:

'It is true.'

'And did I ravish you?' asked Kouame, half crazed.

'No one has ever ravished me, nor will they ever,' Samilia replied.

Sango Kerim's face was quite transfigured. He was paralysed by an icy rage. He could neither move nor speak. Kouame went on, increasingly heated.

'Do you understand, Sango Kerim? She will never belong to either of us, and we shall continue this massacre. This is the only way out. She should kill herself. She should do as her father did.'

Sango Kerim then turned his horse towards Samilia and spoke to her before the crowd of astonished warriors.

'All this time I have fought for you,' he said, 'to stay

faithful to our oath of days gone by, to give you my name, my bed and the city of Massaba. I raised an army of nomads for you, and each of those men, out of friendship for me, agreed to come and die in this place. Today I learn that you gave yourself to Kouame. That he has had the pleasure of you. So yes, I stand alongside him and, like him, I shall ask for your death. Look at all these men, look at these two armies combined here, and tell yourself that with one sweep of your hand you can spare their lives. Even sullied in this way, I will not agree to abandon you to Kouame. But if you kill yourself you belong to no one. And at the very moment that your mind takes wing and your hair is bathed in blood, you will hear the cheers of all these warriors whose lives you have saved.'

Kouame smiled like a madman as Sango Kerim spoke. He hurried up and down the ranks of his army and asked them all: 'Do you want her to die? Do you want her to die?' and more and more voices on both sides started to cry: 'Yes. Let her die.' There were dozens of voices, then hundreds, then the entire army. It was as if these men had suddenly found new hope. They looked upon that small, motionless body, dressed in black, and they understood that she need only disappear for everything to cease. Then, yes, they all bellowed. Louder and louder. They were all shouting, gleefully. Furiously. Yes, Samilia must die. And every-thing could come to an end.

With a flick of his hand, Sango Kerim restored the silence and everyone then turned to that solitary figure. Very slowly, she raised her veil. Every warrior could see the face of the woman for whom they had been dying for so long. She was beautiful. She spoke, and the sands of that plain remember her words to this day.

'You wish me dead,' she said. 'Here, before your men all gathered together, you wish to bring an end to this war. So be it. Cut my throat, then, and seal your peace. And if neither of you has the courage, let a man from the ranks step forward to do what his commander dares not do. I am alone before thousands of men, surrounded. I shall not flee, and if I struggle it will not take long to overpower me. Come on. I am here. Let one of you descend upon me, and be done with it all. But no, you do not move. You say nothing. That is not what you wish for. You want me to kill myself. And you dare to ask me directly to do so. Never. Do you hear me? I asked for nothing. You came before my father, first with gifts, then with armies. War erupted. What have I gained? Nights of mourning, lines on my face and some dust. No, I shall never do as you ask. I do not wish to leave this life. It has given me nothing. I was rich, now my city has been destroyed. I was happy, now my father and brother are buried. I gave myself to Kouame, yes, on the eve of the day which, had Mazehbu not come, would have seen the fall of Massaba. And if I did so, it was because the man who came before me on that night was already dead. I made love to him as you would stroke the forehead of a dead man, that he might smell the fragrance of this life for as long as possible as he made his way into the shadows. You come here, Kouame, and reveal this before the whole army. But it was not to you that I gave myself. It was to your vanquished shade. May you be cursed, both of you, for wanting me to kill myself. And you, my brothers, you say nothing. You had not one word to set against these two cowards. I can see from your eyes that you consent to my death. You hope for it. May you too be cursed, by King Tsongor, your father. Listen well to what Samilia has to say. I shall never turn a knife on my own flesh. If you wish to see me die, strike me yourselves and soil your hands. I have more to say. From this day forward I shall belong to no one. I spit on you, Sango Kerim, and on our childhood memories. I spit on you, Kouame, and on the mother who brought you into this world. I spit on you, my brothers, as you destroy each other with loathing in your entrails. I offer you another solution to stop the war. I shall belong to no one from now. Should you even drag me by the hair, you would not succeed in taking me to your beds. Now there is nothing to force you into war. From this day forward, it will no longer be for me that you are fighting.'

In the stillness and the silence Samilia turned, without even looking at her brothers, turned her back on both armies and left. She was alone. With nothing. She left her life behind her. Kouame and Sango Kerim were preparing to go after her when a strange cry held them back. A cry that rose from the ranks of Kouame's army, powerful but hoarse, a voice that seemed to come from distant centuries.

'Son of a she-dog, at last I have found you. May your name be borne by a succession of corpses!'

Everyone looked to see whence the voice came and to whom it was addressed. Men turned in every direction. Before they knew who was speaking in this way, a prodigious war cry rang out and they saw Arkalas, like an arrow, hurtling out of the ranks. Arkalas, the mad warrior, whose voice no one had recognized because he had not spoken for so long. Bandiagara stood there, beside Sango Kerim. Arakalas had taken some time to recognize him. Much time had passed since that blood-soaked day when, bewitched by Bandiagara's spell, he had methodically massacred all his men. He had suddenly seen it all again in his disturbed mind. And it was then that he had spoken out. In a moment he was upon his enemy. Before anyone had time to make a move he had leapt from his horse and locked onto Bandiagara's face with the voracity of a vampire bat. He ate his face like a frenzied hyena. He made great holes in it with his eager teeth. His nose. His cheeks. He ripped at everything.

Panic swept through the warriors. Arkalas dragged both armies in his wake, and the mêlée began once more. Kouame and Sango Kerim could not set off in pursuit of Samilia. In no time there were dozens of men thronging around them and they were forced to do battle, assailed once again from all quarters, unable to escape the jaws of war. Samilia disappeared, slowly, behind the last of the hills.

The battle lasted all day. When the armies drew apart Sango Kerim and Kouame were haggard with exhaustion and covered in blood. On that night no one found any sleep. Not in the city, nor among the nomad tents. Terrible screams rang out in the darkness all night, the disfigured screams of Bandiagara. He lay there in the middle of the plain, still clinging to life. Arkalas bent over him. He had extricated him from the mêlée to devote himself completely to his torture, and now that the plain was empty he had come back like a dog tugging at his corpse. They could not be seen, but Bandiagara's plaintive wails could be heard, mingled with his torturer's carnivorous laughter. Arkalas continued to tear him to pieces, one shred at a time. Bandiagara's body was one mauled wound, seeping tears. A thousand times he begged his killer to end it and a thousand times Arkalas roared with laughter and drove his teeth back into his body.

With the first glow of light he died at last. It was a hunk of open meat, an unrecognizable mass, that Arkalas left to the insects. From that day forward his teeth would always be red with blood, in remembrance of his carnivorous revenge.

THE CONSTRUCTION OF THE TOMB of Turtles was the slowest and most trying of all. The stench made the days interminably long. The workers toiled without enthusiasm. They were building something ugly, and this weighed heavily on them.

When the tomb was finished Souba left that region and strayed once more along the roadways of the kingdom. He did not know where he should now go. The Tomb of Turtles had called the whole undertaking back into question. It was impossible to create a portrait of his father. At heart, what did he know of the man Tsongor had been? The more he travelled the kingdom, the less able he felt to answer that question. He saw these vast cities surrounded by powerful walls, these paved roads linking one region to the other. He saw bridges and aqueducts, and he knew that all this was the work of Tsongor. But the more he discovered about the vastness of the kingdom, the more clearly he grasped the savage, implacable force necessary to impose such power. He had heard Tsongor's victories presented as heroic legends. He now saw that his father's life had been made of furious determination and sweat. Subjugating entire regions.

Besieging opulent cities to the point of suffocating them. Massacring those who would not yield. Decapitating ageing sovereigns. Souba journeyed up and down the kingdom and realized that he knew nothing of the young Tsongor, of what he had done, of what he had inflicted on others and of what he himself had suffered. He tried to imagine the man who had led his army for all those years of conquest, led it beyond the point of exhaustion. That was the Tsongor only Katabolonga had known.

He needed a site which would say all these things at once. A site which spoke of the king, the conqueror, the father and the killer. A site which spoke of Tsongor's most intimate secrets, his fears, longings and crimes. But there was surely not a site such as that to be found in the entire kingdom.

Souba felt overwhelmed by the scale of his task. For the first time he felt he might spend his entire life looking, and would die having found nothing.

It was then that, in the course of his wanderings, he came to the Hills of the Two Suns. At the close of day the earth in this place seemed to sparkle with light. The sun was setting slowly and the hills lit up with a warm glow. A number of villages seemed to float in the light. Souba stopped to contemplate the beautiful scenery. He

was at the top of a hill. It was still hot, with that voluptuous heat of late afternoon. Before him, just a few paces
away, a tall cypress tree rose up from the ground, solitary and motionless. Souba did not take another step.
He wanted to let this moment wash over him.

'It is here,' he thought. 'Here, at the foot of the
cypress. Quite simply. There is no need for anything else.
A man's tomb, with the light flowing right through it.
Here, yes. Without touching a thing.' He did not take
another step. He felt at home. Everything seemed familiar to him. He thought for a long time but an idea gradually germinated within him and tormented him. No.
This could not be fitting for Tsongor. This humility, this
self-effacement was not in his likeness. It was not Tsongor
who should be buried here but himself, Souba, the son
whose life was spent wandering. Yes. He was now sure
of it. It was here that he was to be buried on the day of
his death. Everything told him so.

He slowly dismounted his mule and walked over to
the cypress. He knelt and his lips kissed the ground. Then
he took a handful of earth and put it into one of the
amulets he wore about his neck. He wanted to carry with
him the smell of the earth from the Hills of the Two
Suns, this earth which would one day provide him with
the ultimate hospitality. He stood back up and whispered
to the hills and the light:

'It is here that I wish to be buried. I do not know when I shall die, but today I have found the place of my death. It is here. I shall not forget it. It is here that I shall return on the very last day.'

Then, when the sun had set at last, he climbed back into the saddle and went on his way. He now knew what he had to do. He had found the place of his death. So it must be for every man. Every man had a part of the earth that waited for him, an adoptive earth into which he might melt. It was the same for Tsongor. Somewhere, there was a site that bore his likeness. He had only to journey on. He would find it eventually. There was nothing to be gained from building tombs. He would never succeed in building a true and complete portrait of his father. He had to journey. The site did exist. He held his amulet tightly. He had found the earth that would cover him. He now had to find Tsongor's earth. It would be self-evident. He could feel it. Self-evident. And his task would be accomplished.

Chapter VI

THE FINAL
RESTING PLACE

As he journeyed on through the kingdom, Souba, still in the saddle, looked upon his hands. The leather strap of the reins hung between his fingers. A thousand tiny lines had appeared on those fingers. Time had passed and his hands bore its mark. He was becoming hypnotized by his own solitude. He sat in his saddle in this way all day, with his head lowered, forgetting to stop, forgetting to eat, absorbed by the idea that, if he remained alone, his life would be spent in this saddle without his achieving his mission. The kingdom was vast. He did not know where to look. He had heard tell of the Oracle of the Sulphurous Lands, and decided he should find this oracle.

The very next morning he headed for the Sulphurous Lands and soon found himself in a landscape of jagged rocks, lent a yellow colour by the sulphur. Plumes of vapour escaped from the rocks. The land looked volcanic, ready to open up at any moment and release towering jets of lava. The oracle was there, in the heart of this arid landscape. The oracle was a woman, sitting on the bare earth. Her face was hidden by a featureless wooden mask. Her breasts swung between the heavy, worn old necklaces that hung from her neck.

Souba sat down facing her. He wanted to give his name and to ask the question which had brought him here but, with a wave of her hand, she bid him not to speak. She handed him a bowl and he drank of what was in it. She fingered a collection of small bones and burned tree roots, rubbing them together. She invited him to smear grease over his face and hands. At last he felt that he could ask his question.

'My name is Souba. I am the son of Tsongor. I am searching through my father's vast kingdom for a site in which to bury him. A site where the earth is waiting for him. I search but I find nothing.'

At first the oracle gave no reply. The aged woman drank from the bowl herself and spat the liquid back out in a great spout which evaporated in the air. Only then did Souba hear her voice, a shrill, harsh voice which made the ground around him tremble.

'You shall find what you seek,' she said, 'only when you yourself are a Tsongor. Only when you are ashamed of yourself.'

She looked Souba right in the eye and started to laugh as she said once more:

'Ashamed, yes. I shall help you in that. You shall know shame, believe me.'

Still she laughed. Souba sat open-mouthed. He felt anger rising within him. The aged woman had not answered his question. Her laughter, her yellow teeth – everything about her was an insult. She was laughing at him. His father was King Tsongor. There was no shame for him to recognize. It was not shame that the Tsongors handed from father to son. Everything she implied was absurd and insulting. A mad old woman laughing at him. He thought of rising to his feet and leaving but he wanted to ask another question. He forced himself to remain seated and spoke again. He wanted to have news of his city. Of Massaba, of course, he had had word. But it was always in the same terms: 'They are still fighting there.' The rumours said nothing else. No details reached him now. There was no one left to say who had launched the latest attack and who had repelled it. It was war, and he knew nothing more. He asked the oracle for news of those he loved and, once again, she spat an arc of the blue liquid which evaporated. Then she bellowed into his face:

'Dead. They are all dead. Your brother Liboko first. Like a rat. The others will follow. They will all die. Each in turn, like rats. One by one.'

And once again her face twisted with laughter. Souba was devastated. He blocked his ears that he might not hear any longer, but the very stones seemed to laugh beneath him. He could not escape the aged woman's cackling. He imagined his brother Liboko, lying lifeless in the dust. And so anger swept over him. He leapt to his feet, grasped a heavy, gnarled stick and brought it crashing down on the oracle with all his might. A dull thud reverberated through the rocks. He had struck her full on the head. The laughing stopped. The body fell with all its weight. Inert. Souba heard nothing now. Saw nothing now. He held the stick tightly in his hands. The anger was still in him. Liboko. His brothers. He struck once more. He struck again and again. Then at last, breathless, sweating, he dropped the stick and regained his senses. A lump of flesh lay at his feet. Lifeless. He was gripped with terror and fled.

He spurred his mule's flanks although he did not know where to go. He could not rid himself of the aged woman's face. He had killed her. For no reason. For her laughter. Out of anger. He had killed her. That laughter. That voice. That silent force burgeoning within him, like a wave washing over him. He had killed her. He had this in him, a furious passion powerful enough to kill. Murder in his blood. He was a Tsongor. He too was capable of this.

For several days he allowed the mule to carry him, unable to choose a direction, wandering wherever the tracks took him. His hands shook. He had left the stick behind. He no longer spoke a word. An immense weariness swept through him. Violence was within him. He had experienced it. It was the savage violence of the Tsongors, the violence which flowed in his brothers' blood. Yes, he had given himself up to the voluptuous rapture of anger. He had killed the oracle. He now knew he was no better than his brothers. He too could kill for Massaba. And only his father's command kept him away from the carnage and the fever of the fray.

He drifted along the roads, not eating, not stopping, exhausted by his weariness and by the horror. He drifted, head lowered, instinctively fleeing any form of life. He wanted to be alone, invisible. It seemed to him that his crime could be read upon his hands. Sometimes he wept, whispering: 'I am a Tsongor. I am a Tsongor. Do not come near me.'

SAMILIA HAD LEFT MASSABA. LIKE a captive fleeing, taking nothing with her. For the first few days she thought she would have to do battle, and she prepared herself for this. Sango Kerim and Kouame would not be long in catching up with her and she would be forced, once again, to scream at them to leave her alone. She was determined. She would yield nothing more. But time passed and neither Sango Kerim nor Kouame came. Clearly, no one was following her. She had been right. She meant nothing any more. In the beginning it had been for her that war was declared. But from the first life lost, from the first man whose death must be avenged, she had no longer fuelled the fighting. Blood called for more blood and the pretenders had eventually forgotten her. No one was following her, no one but the wind and the hills.

Life for her then became nothing more than a long nomadic wandering. She went from village to village, living only on alms. Along the roads of the kingdom peasants stopped digging the land to watch this strange horsewoman pass by. They looked upon this woman in black who rode with her head lowered. No one came near. She crossed whole countries without speaking a word. Without ever asking anything of this life other than the strength to continue. She aged along the roads, always riding on straight ahead. She eventually reached the furthest limits of the kingdom. And, without even realizing it, without a backward glance at the continent she left behind, she passed that last frontier and drove on into the unexplored lands. She went further even than King Tsongor had in his younger days, leaving the native lands of the kingdom and their faded taste to evaporate behind her. She no longer had a name, or a past. To those who met her she was a strange figure whom people barely dared to address and whom they watched passing with the obscure feeling that there was in her something violent, something best avoided. They prayed that she might not stop. And Samilia never stopped. She rode on, obstinately, along the roads and the tracks. Until all she was to anyone was a dot vanishing in the distance.

KOUAME AND SANGO KERIM HAD become two dried-out shadows, their bodies exhausted. Their minds had begun to falter when Samilia had left. They no longer thought of anything. No longer wished for anything. They wanted only to bite and bring blood forth from the earth. All those years of warfare were culminating in this. They had killed so many men and hoped for so much, and all that was left to them now were the memories of battles over which they wept. Dogs seemed to laugh at them as they saw them pass. The madness which, thus far, had merely nibbled at their flesh now washed right over them.

Of Massaba, there was nothing left. The city had been destroyed from the inside out. The houses had collapsed, dismantled stone by stone to fill the holes in the city walls. The once proud buildings were now shapeless. All that was left was the outer wall protecting a collection of ruins from attack. Dust had replaced the paving-stones. The fruit trees had been felled and burned. Samilia had left. And, as the fighting came to a close, the battle was lost. For everyone.

* * *

And so, one last time, Kouame and Sango Kerim regrouped their armies on the plain and, one last time, they addressed each other.

'This is the end,' said Sango Kerim. 'You know it as well as I, Kouame. All that is left for us to do is to finish what has been started. There are still men destined to die who are not yet fallen. Neither you nor I can eclipse ourselves from this final mêlée. But I wish to proclaim here the terms for the last day, after which I shall be silent and shall know only death and fury. Before our two armies gathered here, I say this: That those who wish to leave should do so this day. You have all fought honourably. The war ends on this day. From this day forward, vengeance begins. Let those who have a home to which to go, go. Let those who have a wife who waits for them leave this moment. Let those who have the death of no one beloved to avenge lay down their arms. For them, everything ends this day. They will have gained none of the riches they may have hoped for here, but they will leave with their lives. May they cherish them jealously. As for the rest, let them prepare to go into the final fray. There will be no respite now. We shall fight day and night. We shall fight without thinking of Massaba and its treasures. We shall fight to avenge ourselves.'

'What you say is good and just, Sango Kerim,' replied Kouame. 'This war will not go beyond this day. What is to ensue is the carnage of the demented. Let those who still can leave, without shame, and go back whence they came to spread word of what we have been.'

In the ranks of the warriors there was a long, uneasy silence. The men looked at each other. No one dared move. No one dared be the first to leave. It was then that Rassamilagh spoke.

'I am leaving, Sango Kerim. It is a long time since we lost this war. And for a long time I have been rising each morning as a vanquished man. I regret that night on which we drank the spirit of sand myrtles, and on which everything could have ceased. I have been beside you everywhere. Everything you endured, I endured. Today I turn to peace. If any man here wishes to make me pay for the death of a brother or a friend, I shall confront him. But if no man comes forward, I shall leave and I shall bury the war of Massaba in the sands of my past.'

No one moved. Slowly, Rassamilagh left the ranks. This marked the beginning of a large exodus. In each camp, from every tribe, men reached their decision. The young because they still had years to live before them and they wanted to see their families again. The old because they were gripped by the stubborn desire to be buried in their own land. Men clasped each other to their breasts in every direction. Those who were leaving bid adieu to those who stayed. They took them in their arms, recommending them to the earth. They offered them their weapons, their helmets and their mounts. But those who were staying wanted nothing. It was they, in fact, who wanted to give their belongings away. They said that, for them, the end was near and that soon they would have no need of anything but the golden coin slipped between a dead man's teeth. To those who left they entrusted their belongings, their amulets and messages to convey. It was like a large body slowly carving itself up. In places the ranks were much depleted.

At last those who were leaving were ready. They left the plain that very day. They had to be far from there once battle commenced, lest the sight of their companions caught up in torment should call them back to arms.

There was but a handful of men left on the plain. The madmen burned by war, those prepared to embrace vengeance. Each of them still had a man to kill. Each wanted to avenge a brother or a friend, and stared with a dog's savage loathing at whomsoever they intended to attack.

Old Barnak was there. Those of his companions who had decided to leave had laid at his feet their reserves of khat. There was so much of it that it formed a great heap of dried weed. Slowly he leant forward, took a whole handful of khat and put it into his mouth. He chewed it, spat it back out, leant forward again and took another handful of weed. When he had spat it all back out, all that was left were the ends of the chewed roots. He muttered to himself:

'Now I shall never sleep again.'

No man had ever swallowed such a quantity of the drug. His entire body was racked with twitches and jerks. His muscles, wearied by the years, once again had the vigour of a serpent. The visions assailing him made his eyes roll and his mouth foam. He was ready.

The signal was given and the fray commenced. One last assault of the frenzied few who remained. There was no strategy now, no fraternity. Every man fought for himself, not to preserve his life, but to take that of the enemy he had designated for himself. It was like a mêlée of wild boars. Streams of blood flooded over faces. Armour was caved in. A horrible chorus of death rattles made the immutable old walls of Massaba tremble.

Sango Kerim and Kouame were the first to launch themselves at each other. There in the midst of the confusion, each tried with all his might to pierce the other's flanks. But once again neither succeeded in vanquishing the other. Beads of sweat formed on their brows. In vain they exhausted themselves in battle. It was then that Barnak loomed beside them. With a sweep of his arm he decapitated Sango Kerim. His head rolled pitifully across the sand and he did not even have time to bid farewell to the city he had seen being conceived and built. The life was already flowing out of him. Kouame lowered his sword. He could not countenance it. His enemy lay at his feet. But he did not have time to revel in this victory. Old Barnak was now looking on him with his drug-maddened eyes. He no longer recognized anyone. All about him, all he saw were bodies to slash and pierce. He drove his sword right up to the hilt into Kouame's neck, and Kouame's eyes stared into his, wide with astonishment. He slumped to the ground. Lifeless. Killed by his friend, at the feet of his decapitated rival.

Barnak was then attacked by dozens of warriors, from both camps. They circled him like huntsmen cornering a wild beast and weakening it with their blows. He died thus, struck by dozens of lances. Trampled and stoned by two armies combined.

Warriors fell in every direction. In every direction the bodies piled up. Slowly all resources were exhausted. All that remained were the hideously wounded who dragged themselves away in an effort to escape the feasting hyenas already thronging over the plain. Sako was the last to die. His brother Danga opened his belly and spread his entrails on the ground. In a last effort he managed to strike a blow at Danga's foot. Blood sprang out from the severed tendon but Danga laughed. He had won.

'You are dying, Sako, and victory is mine. Mine too is Massaba and our father's kingdom. You are dying. I struck you down.'

He left his brother's body and wanted to run to Massaba. To open the gates of the city as its master. To enjoy his prize. But the blood continued to flow from his wound. He could no longer walk and grew steadily weaker. The city then seemed infinitely far from him. He was crawling now. Still laughing. He could not see that the prediction was being fulfilled. He, Sako's twin, born two hours after his brother, was to die two hours after him. Sako had preceded him in death and he was waiting for him, impatiently. Slowly Danga was emptying of his blood. And, as he had been born, propelled into the sheets bathed by the blood of his brother's birth, so he was to die in the dust reddened by carnage. Everything had been fulfilled. The death of one marked for the other the term of his own life.

* * *

When Danga expired, having failed to reach the gates of the city, a vast silence descended on Massaba. There was no one left. The hour had come for carrion eaters and the heavy flight of vultures.

'DO YOU NOT WEEP, TSONGOR?'

Katabolonga's voice echoed in the vast underground hall of the sepulchre. The corpse gave no reply.

'Do you not weep, Tsongor?' Katabolonga asked again.

Tsongor heard his friend's distant voice but gave no reply. No, he did not weep. And yet he saw them pass. All his children. All the warriors of Massaba. The final combatants. There they were, before his eyes. Their faces shattered. Their eyes wearied by years of war. There they were, moving slowly and steadily, a cortège of the dead. He could see Kouame and Sango Kerim. He saw his two sons, Sako and Danga, still clinging to each other. They were all there. Tsongor did not weep. No. It was to him as if he were watching a procession of madmen. Thirsting for blood. He remained quite motionless, and did not even try to call to them. He felt nothing but contempt for these warriors who had killed each other down to the last man. No, he did not weep. As the dead passed before him, they sensed his presence and lowered their heads. Tsongor was there, judging them with his patriarch's eye. Tsongor let them pass before him without attempting to speak, without attempting to take them in his arms and kiss them, one last time, on the temples. And so they were gripped by their shame. They headed for the shore with nothing more to hope for. Tsongor watched them disappear. They were all there. He looked carefully upon every body. Every face. He was now quite sure that Samilia was not among them. His anger grew greater still. And now he spoke to the damned with his voice of stone, with all the wrath of a father scorned.

'You had no right,' he said. 'No right to die. Samilia is alive. You have left her alone. You claimed to be fighting for her. You tore each other down to the very last man and you have forgotten her. There is no one left to watch over her. May you all be cursed. You had no right.'

The troop disappeared slowly. Not one of them dared turn to look. Tsongor stayed there, the only shade unable to make the crossing. A distant voice called him back to the land of the living. He recognized it. It was the voice of Katabolonga.

'Do you not weep, Tsongor?'

No. He did not weep. He clenched his fists with rage, cursing the damned.

SOUBA CONTINUED TO STRAY ALONG the pathways of the kingdom, but his demeanour had changed. He was like a fearful shadow. He avoided towns, kept himself apart from habitation. He was haunted, every moment, by the murder of the oracle. His shame gave him no respite. He thought of his father, of his conquests and his crimes. He now felt that he understood him. He thought again of the oracle's words. Yes, she had been right. He felt only disgust for himself. He no longer thought of the tombs. The very idea of overseeing another construction was appalling to him. No, he would not build this last tomb. He wanted to flee, to eclipse himself from the world. He was a danger to all men. His hands were capable of killing. He headed slowly, as slowly as an old man, towards the Great Gorges of the North, those steep, lofty mountains, wild and abandoned by mankind. Only there would he be able to hide himself. Only there would no one come to find him. He wanted to disappear, and the Great Gorges seemed to him the perfect labyrinth in which to lose himself.

When he arrived he stood speechless before the prodigious spectacle of these mountains. It was a rugged landscape: long gorges carved through it like thin pathways of stone, corridors barely wide enough to allow a single man to pass. Nothing here was on the human scale. Sometimes, after following one of these gorges, he would arrive at a great plateau, like a terrace. As far as the eye could see there was only the vast silence of the mountains. For the first time since the murder of the oracle he felt appeased. Occasionally a buzzard would tear through the silence of the skies. He was alone in a wild world. He allowed his mule to carry him forwards.

For three days he strayed through this maze of stone, trusting himself to the whims of his mount. Without drinking or eating, like a shadow slowly dying, carried by the wind. On the fourth day, when his strength had left him, he suddenly came upon the entrance to a palace carved into the rock. He believed at first it was a hallucination, but the entrance was indeed there. Austere yet sumptuous. It was here that Tsongor should be buried. He knew this immediately. He stepped down from his mule and knelt before the palace. Here. Perhaps Tsongor himself had built this palace. Perhaps he had come to this place and had felt here what Souba had felt beside the cypress in the Hills of the Two Suns. Or perhaps this silent palace, not known to any man, had existed for all eternity. Forgotten by all men. Yes, it was here that Tsongor must be buried, in a majestic and regal tomb, sumptuous but hidden, that no man would ever find. It was here that Tsongor should rest. The mountains matched his stature. He could hide his shame among them. Souba was in no doubt now. A land which was not on the human scale, infinitely more beautiful and more wild, a land beyond the limits of this world. He had found it.

When he settled back into the saddle he knew that his journey was over. It only remained for him to return to Massaba. He had built six tombs throughout the kingdom, and had found the seventh, Tsongor's final resting place. It only remained to bury him, that he might at last rest in peace.

NOT A WHISPER, NOT ONE sound of battle now troubled the king's deep sleep. Tsongor and Katabolonga no longer talked. There was nothing more to say. Yet the aged king was still restless. Katabolonga thought that this was due once again to the rusted coin. That Tsongor was once more harrowed by the desire to reach the other shore of the dead. But one day, at last, he spoke, and his voice had not echoed through the hall for so long that Katabolonga jumped like a frightened monkey.

'To my sons,' said Tsongor, 'I bequeathed my empire. They tore it to pieces with their teeth and killed each other over a heap of ruins. I do not weep for them. But what did I bequeath to Samilia? Neither the husband I promised her, nor the life to which she had a right. Where is she now? Of Samilia I know nothing. She was my only daughter and has had nothing of myself. To Souba I have perhaps passed on what I am. But Samilia is the element that has escaped me. And yet it was for her that I so carefully prepared my legacy. I wanted to give her a man. Lands. I wanted my life to have served this purpose. To ensure that she was sheltered, safe. That nothing could harm her, ever. That my shade, her father's shade, should watch over her and her descendants. I have bequeathed her only mourning. Mourning for her father, and then mourning for her brothers, one after the other, in succession; the deaths of the pretenders to her hand; the sacking of her city. What has she had from me? Promises of feasting and celebrations, and the ashes of ransacked houses. Samilia is the one who has been sacrificed. I did not wish for that. No one wished for it. But everyone has forgotten her.'

Tsongor fell silent. Katabolonga gave no reply. He had nothing to say. He too had often thought of Samilia. He had wondered, sometimes, whether it was his duty to try to find her, to escort her wherever she went, watching over her. But he had done nothing. He felt, despite his compassion for her, that it was not his place. His loyalty lay in waiting for Souba. There should be nothing other than this. And so, like all the others, he had left Samilia to disappear. And, like all the others, he carried the remorse for this within him. For he felt that this woman was sacred. Sacred for what she had lived. Sacred because each of them, one by one, and without even realizing they were doing so, had sacrificed her.

SOUBA BEGAN TO JOURNEY BACK. He rode for weeks on end, impatient to see the land of his birth and anxious as to what he might find there. His mule had aged. She covered the ground more slowly. She had become almost blind, but still led him across the roadways of the kingdom, unhesitating. On her saddle the eight plaits of the women of Massaba still hung, bleached white by the passing years. They were Souba's sand-glass, measuring time. A whole lifetime had passed. He arrived on the crest of the tallest of the seven hills at dawn. Massaba was at his feet. It struck him immediately that the great city had been reduced to a paltry heap of stone. Only the fortified walls still retained their imposing outline. The plain was empty. Gone were the tented villages that once clustered at the feet of the city. He could no longer even distinguish any trace of the roadways that once thronged with bustling vendors. There was nothing left. Souba climbed slowly down onto the plain and entered the city of Massaba.

It was a deserted city. Not a sound. Nothing moving among these impassive stones. Everything had crumbled.

Those inhabitants who survived the long years of war had all eventually fled this accursed place. They had left everything as it was: the open squares, the houses half destroyed. Time and vegetation had taken it over. Green moss now covered every façade. Tall weeds had grown up in the courtyards and the terraces, between the tiles on the roofs and in the cracks in the walls of houses. It was as if Massaba had been slowly consumed by plants. Ivy gnawed through the houses that remained standing. The wind slammed doors and raised a thick layer of dust. Souba walked up and down the streets of the city with his jaw clenched. Massaba had not fallen. No, it had rotted slowly. The streets were strewn with the vestiges of the fighting they had seen: fragments of helmets. Shards of glass. A few charred remains of machines of war.

Everything flooded through his mind: the faces of those he had left behind; the company of his brothers; that last evening they had spent together, the eve of his departure; the singing; the spirits they had drunk that night. He remembered his sister's hand stroking his arm. He remembered the tears he had shed. He was alone in knowing that all that had once existed. His mule paced on through the desolation and he felt as if he were several centuries old. In his mind's eye he saw a world that had now disappeared. He trailed up and down the streets

234

already submerged in the past. He was like a dazed survivor, watching a whole generation of men die and being left all alone, aghast, in a world that has no name.

When he stepped into old Tsongor's palace, a strong smell leapt up at him. A colony of monkeys had taken up residence in the vast halls of the palace. There were hundreds of them. Thousands. They had covered the carpets with their excrement. They leapt from one room to the next, swinging on the chandeliers. Souba had to force a path through them, pushing them aside with his feet. They were howler monkeys. Their shrill cries were the only sound that now rose up from the city. An animal cry, inarticulate. Sometimes they shrieked like this for nights on end, a piercing concert which made the very walls of the palace shudder.

Souba went down into the great hall where his father lay. It was dark. He stepped forward slowly, feeling his way, tripping several times. It was then that he heard a loud crack from the middle of the hall. This was followed by a sudden blaze of light which blinded him. A torch had been lit.

He flattened himself against the wall for a moment,

gripped by fear. He gradually identified the tomb on which his father lay. Above him stood a creature whose face was now lit by the torch.

'Tsongor is waiting for you, Souba.'

He recognized that voice at once. It was as if he had left him only the day before. The man who stood before him was Katabolonga, bearer of his father's golden footstool. He was as emaciated as a sacred cow, cheeks hollowed by the passage of time. A huge beard hid his face, and he was filthy. But he stood erect, to the full impressive height of the Men who Crawl. For all these years he had fed on the monkeys that had ventured as far as this room. Not moving once. Staying beside the body. Souba was overcome by a feeling of great joy. There was still one man who knew the world into which he had been born. Who remembered his brothers' faces, knew how beautiful Samilia was, and how magnificent the fountains of Massaba had been. There was still that. Here, amid the monkey bones gnawed in the darkness, there was still a man who had waited for him and could speak his name.

Together they honoured the promise made to Tsongor. Carefully, they lifted the king's body and brought it back up to the surface. There they built a stretcher of wood which they harnessed to the aged mule. And, once again, Souba set out along the roads.

They left the city which had once been queen, left it for ever, abandoning it to the lichens and the monkeys. They walked on either side of the mule without speaking, each watching over the body of the dead king. Suddenly, just as they reached the top of the hill, they heard the plaintive chorus of the howler monkeys. It was as if the city were bidding them a last farewell. Or like the mocking laughter of fate raising its victory cry, in a land of silence.

SOUBA TOOK HIS FATHER'S BODY to the Crimson Mountains of the North. As they journeyed, Katabolonga told him of what had happened in Massaba. The death of Liboko. The disappearance of Samilia. The inexorable destruction of the city. Souba asked no questions. He did not have the strength. He simply wept. The bearer broke off from his account, then, when the tears had dried, he continued. Thus Souba lived through the death throes of Massaba and of those he loved, from the words of Tsongor's aged servant.

When they reached the Crimson Mountains they made their way through the narrow stone gorges. Katabolonga looked upon this labyrinth of rock, these rugged corridors where the sun barely shed any light, as he would have looked upon a sacred site. There was in the towering outline of those rocks a sense of an eternity held in suspense. No one lived here but a few wild goats and large lizards which sidled from one stone to the next.

After walking through the gorges for an hour they arrived at last at the tomb. The sumptuous façade of the palace rose up before them, carved into the ochre stone.

It seemed to them like a silent door which led to the heart of the mountains.

They lay Tsongor's illustrious body in the last hall within the palace. Souba straightened the dead man's royal tunic with all the attentiveness of a son. He stood in quiet contemplation for a while with his hand on his father's chest. He called on his spirit. Then, when he felt that King Tsongor was there once more, all about him, he spoke into the dead man's ear, saying those words which he had kept in his memory through all those years:

'It is I, father. It is Souba. I am beside you. Hear my voice. I live. Rest in peace. Everything is accomplished.'

He kissed King Tsongor's forehead. And then, very slowly, the corpse smiled. He heard his son's voice. He knew from its register, more mature and deeper than it had been in times gone by, that years had passed. In spite of the war and the massacres, one thing, at least, had come to pass as he had hoped. Souba lived. And he had kept his word. It was time, at last, to leave. Katabolonga came over slowly. From one of the little mahogany boxes that he carried about his neck he took Tsongor's old rusted coin. And carefully, without saying a word, he slipped it between the dead man's teeth. Everything was accomplished. Now that his life had come to term, Tsongor was dying with no treasure but the coin he had taken with him on the eve of his life of conquest. And so King Tsongor's long slow death throes came to an end. He smiled sadly, as one who is tortured and suffering. He smiled as he contemplated the faces of his son and his aged friend, and he died for the second time.

Souba remained beside the body for a long time. He imprinted on his mind his father's last expression. That sad and distant smile that he had never seen him wear in his lifetime. He understood that, for Tsongor, there could be no relief. In spite of his son's return, in spite of the coin from Katabolonga, the aged king had died thinking of Samilia. And this memory would torment him even beyond his death.

Souba lifted the massive slab of marble and sealed the tomb. Everything was finished. He had done what he had to. It was then that Katabolonga turned to him and said gently:

'Go now, Souba, live the life that you must live, and fear nothing. I shall stay beside Tsongor. I am here. I shall not move.'

Before Souba could give any reply, the towering servant with the hollowed face held him to him and waved him away. There was nothing more to say. Souba knew this. He turned and walked towards the entrance to the tomb. Katabolonga watched his silhouette as it receded, reciting prayers between his teeth, prayers recommending Souba to life. He felt death rising within him.

'There,' he thought, 'it is my turn now. I shall go no further. I am the last of the old world. The age of King Tsongor and of Massaba has passed, as has the time allotted to my life. I shall go no further.'

He crouched before the tomb, like a guard, ready to leap, with one hand on the pommel of his dagger and the other holding the sacred golden footstool. And he died. His body hardened like the stone around him and he stayed thus for all eternity, like a vigilant statue forbidding intruders access to this sacred site. There he stayed, Katabolonga. For ever. Head held high and proud. Eyes locked onto the door of the tomb and onto Souba as he disappeared from view.

King Tsongor's son emerged from the vast halls carved into the rock, came back out into the light of day and climbed onto his ageless mule. He trod back along the same route through the tall rocks that watched him in silence. Through all these nights of journeying he had never stopped pondering the same question: why had his father entrusted this task to him? Why had he condemned him to exile and solitude? Far from those he loved, constrained to learn nothing more of Massaba's fate. Why had he chosen him, Souba, the youngest of all? He who had dreamed of quite another life. He who had so often wanted to abandon the seven tombs to go to the aid of Massaba. These questions had often troubled him and he had never been able to find a reply. He had aged. And he had eventually come to view this task as a curse which had banished him from the world and from life. But now, quite suddenly, he understood that, on the terrace in Massaba, during his great sleepless night, his father had foreseen everything. He had seen the terrifying war brewing. He had seen the bloody siege of Massaba and the endless massacres that drenched the plain with blood. He had felt that the world would capsize. That everything would disappear. That nothing would be left and neither he nor anyone else could resist this savage force which bore everything away with it. So he had called for Souba and condemned him to years of wandering and of toil, that, for all that time, he might be kept far from the misery that consumed everything. When all this had come to term, there should be at least one man left. He had been right. There was one man left now. The last survivor of the House of Tsongor.

Souba had acquitted himself of his promise, but Tsongor's sad smile obsessed him. There was still Samilia, whom everyone had forgotten, and who had been devastated by this life. He thought, for a while, that he might set out to find her. But he knew the vastness of the kingdom and he knew he would never find her. That search would indeed be in vain. He thought for a long time as he rode his mule, until he came to the last of the gorges in the Crimson Mountains. He then looked up and contemplated the landscape around him. The mountains were behind him. Before him was the vastness of the kingdom. He was the last of a squandered world. A mature man whose life had not yet begun. It remained for him to live. He smiled. He now knew what he must do. He would build a palace. Until that day he had obeyed his father and erected tombs, one by one. Now it was of Samilia that he must think. He would build a palace. Samilia's palace. An austere but sumptuous edifice which would crown all his work. He would try to match his sister's beauty. He would contrive it so that this palace spoke of both the splendour of her life and the waste of this existence consumed by ill-fortune. Yes, it remained for him to do this. No one would ever step inside Tsongor's tombs. He had sealed them all, one by one, that only the silence of death might reign within them. Samilia's palace would remain open, a princely harbour for travellers. Men from every corner of the kingdom would come there to rest. Women would bring offerings to honour the memory of King Tsongor's daughter. A palace open to the winds of the world, like a caravanserai reverberating with noise and conversation. He would build this palace and perhaps, one day, Samilia would hear tell of it and would come to him. He would build a palace to call his sister. And so be it if she were already too far, beyond the limits of the world. So be it if she was never meant to return. The palace would be there. To tell everyone of the error of the Tsongors. To offer hospitality, for all eternity, to Samilia's wandering sisters, straying like her across the earth. And to honour the memory of Samilia.